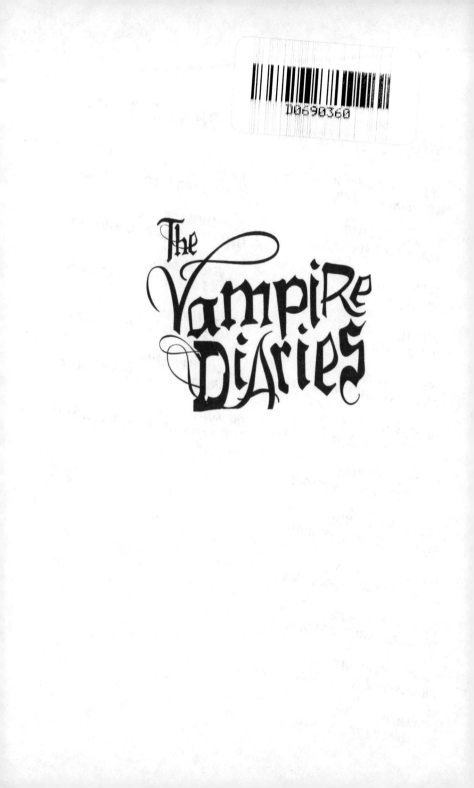

# The Vampire Diaries

# BOOKS IN THE VAMPIRE DIARIES SERIES

CREATED BY
#1 *NEW YORK TIMES*
BESTSELLING AUTHOR

L. J. Smith

WRITTEN BY AUBREY CLARK

The Vampire Diaries

THE SALVATION

VOL. 3

UNMASKED

47NORTH

*The Vampire Diaries: The Salvation: Unmasked © 2014 by L.J. Smith*

**alloyentertainment**

*Produced by Alloy Entertainment*
*1700 Broadway*
*New York, NY 10019*
*www.alloyentertainment.com*

*Library of Congress Catalog Number: 2013958185*

*First edition May 2014*

*Published by 47North, Seattle*
*www.apub.com*

*ISBN 10: 1477823352*
*ISBN 13: 9781477823354*

*Cover design by Liz Dresner*

# A Note About the Hashtags in This Book

Elena's diary may be private, but this book doesn't have to be.
Everyone's talking about the biggest shockers, twists, and swoon-worthy moments.

Look for the hashtags throughout this book and share your own reactions on Twitter. To connect with other readers right now, tag your tweets with #TVD13.

"I'm going to plant the herb garden right there," Bonnie told Zander, gazing out across their new yard. Green grass spread out in front of her, running right to the edge of a winding country road. There was a little space, half in sun and half in shade, that would be perfect for growing herbs for her spells and charms. Beyond the road rose white-topped mountains—*real* mountains, much higher than the rolling hills of Virginia.

Behind her, Zander wrapped his arms around her waist and tucked his chin against her shoulder. Bonnie leaned back comfortably against his warm bulk. Taking a deep, satisfied breath of the crisp Colorado air, she told him, "It's absolutely gorgeous here."

They'd only been here for a few days, and each morning when Bonnie opened her eyes, she was startled by her own happiness. She'd moved here because she couldn't bear to lose Zander, but she had never considered that she might actually like it.

Even on the plane flying here, she'd had an anxious pit in her stomach. Bonnie had never lived so far away from her family before, never spent more than a few months some place where she couldn't drive to her mom or one of her sisters if she needed them. And she'd always had her *other* sisters, the ones she'd chosen, Elena and Meredith, by her side.

Bonnie had felt like a traitor leaving Elena and Meredith. They'd assured her that they understood and reminded her she was only a phone call away. But that didn't relieve Bonnie's guilt. Stefan, Elena's true love, had *died*. Meredith had been turned into a vampire. Surely it was *wrong* for Bonnie to abandon them, especially now.

But being here felt *right*. The Colorado sky stretched bright and blue overhead, so clear and deep that Bonnie almost thought she could hold her arms above her head and fly straight up into its limitless space.

There was something about that endless sky, something about the open country and nature all around her that made Bonnie feel like she was bursting with Power.

"I'm getting stronger every day," she said, twining her fingers with Zander's and pulling his arms tighter around her.

"*Mmhmm*," Zander agreed, kissing her neck softly. "This place is really alive. Jared told me he ran for miles last night in the mountains as a wolf, and there was nothing to avoid, no cars or towns in his way. Pretty cool."

He tugged her around by the hand, and Bonnie followed him into the house. *Our house. How awesome is that?* she thought. She'd liked their old apartments, she guessed, but this little white ranch house had no neighbors to complain about noise, no landlord laying down rules. It was *theirs*.

"We can do anything we want here," she told Zander.

He grinned down at her with his slow, devastating smile. "And what is it that you want to do, Miss Bonnie?"

Bonnie's face widened in a mischievous grin. "Oh, I've got a few ideas," she said lightly, and went up on her tiptoes to kiss him, her eyes fluttering closed.

The same familiar zing that Zander's kisses always gave her was there, but with something extra: They were *married* now. Till death do us part. He was hers.

She opened her eyes and looked up into Zander's warm, ocean-blue ones. A thrill of happiness shot through her. Channeling a shred of Zander's energy into herself, Bonnie concentrated for a moment. Joy shot through her as she felt the essence of her sweet, cheerful husband. In the fireplace, violet and green sparks flew, filling the space with light and color.

"Beautiful," Zander said. "Like tiny fireworks."

Bonnie was about to say something cheesy but honest, something like, *That's how I feel with you all the time—fireworks.* But before she could, her phone rang.

*Meredith.* Her friend no doubt wanted to know how the honeymoon had been and what Colorado was like. Bonnie answered, still smiling, "Hey! What's up?"

There was a pause. Then, Meredith's voice, thin and ragged. "Bonnie?"

"Meredith?" Bonnie stiffened. Her friend sounded *broken.*

"It's Elena," Meredith said, almost too quietly for Bonnie to hear. "Can you come home?"

\* \* \*

Sitting on the edge of Elena's bed, Damon closed his eyes, just for a moment. He was so tired, a bone-deep exhaustion worse than any he could remember feeling before. He'd sat by Elena's bedside for hours, her hand in his, silently willing her to keep breathing, and her heart to keep pounding.

Willing Elena to wake up.

And she'd kept breathing, somehow, although each slow, rattling breath seemed like it would be her last. All the way across the Atlantic from Paris, back to her home here in Virginia, she'd kept breathing. He could hear her heart beating, but weakly and irregularly.

But still, she was unconscious. It didn't matter how hard Damon willed her to wake up. It didn't matter if he pleaded with Elena herself, or if he pulled out all the half-forgotten prayers of his childhood and begged a god who he was sure had turned away from him long ago.

Nothing Damon did mattered.

Gently, he brushed back a long strand of Elena's hair from her cheek. The once bright gold was duller now, tangled and matted, and her cheeks were sallow. She looked so close to death that Damon's heart clenched.

Lifting his hand away from Elena's face, Damon pressed his fist briefly against his chest. There was a dull empty ache there, where he was used to feeling Elena's emotions running bright and strong through the bond between them. He hadn't felt anything from their bond since Elena had fallen unconscious.

"Come as fast as you can," he heard Meredith say in the living room. On the other end of the phone line, he could hear Bonnie's distressed voice promising to drop everything, to catch the first plane out. When Meredith finally hung up, there was a moment of pure silence before she gave a tearful sniff.

She was pinning her hopes on the little redbird's magic, he knew. Damon couldn't help a traitorous little spark of hope himself—Bonnie was so Powerful now—but, deep inside, he knew that even Bonnie wouldn't be able to help.

The Guardians had made up their minds, and Elena was doomed.

Damon stood and paced across the bedroom to stare out of the open window. Outside, the sun was setting. The bedroom's walls pressed in around him. He was achingly conscious of Elena, lying silent and still behind him.

Enough. He could sit by her bedside as long as he liked, but he wasn't helping her. Damon was *useless*. He had to get out of here, away from Elena's shallow breaths and the faint, dreadful scent of death that was slowly filling the room.

Damon concentrated and felt his body compact, his bones twisting and hollowing. Shining black feathers sprang from his new form. After a few moments, a sleek black crow spread his wings wide and flew through the window and out into the night.

Angling his wings to catch the evening breeze, Damon turned toward the river. Above him, dark gray clouds gathered, mirroring his emotions.

Without consciously directing his flight, he soon found himself above Stefan's grave on the riverbank. Landing and transforming gracefully back to his natural form, Damon looked around. It had only been a few weeks since they'd buried Stefan, but grass had already grown over the earth where his younger brother lay. As Damon gazed at it, the ache in his chest intensified.

He bent and laid one hand against the ground over Stefan's grave. The earth was dry and crumbled under his fingers. "I'm sorry, little brother," he said. "I failed you. I've failed Elena."

Straightening, he wondered what he was doing. Dead was dead. Stefan couldn't forgive him now, as much as it pained Damon to want him to.

They'd spent so much time hating each other. Damon could admit now that it was his fault. He'd resented his younger brother for a host of reasons, beginning with the fact that their father had loved Stefan best. His hatred had intensified after that dreadful day that they'd killed each other, and through centuries of watching from a distance as Stefan suffered through his vampirism and refrained from killing humans, Damon had grown more and more bitter. Even as a monster, Stefan had been more virtuous than Damon had been as a man, and Damon had loathed him for it.

But by the time Jack came along, Damon didn't hate Stefan anymore. *Jack.* Damon's jaw tightened with hatred, and overhead, thunder rumbled in response.

Jack Daltry had pretended to be a human hunting a vicious, ancient vampire. It had all been a lie: Jack was a scientist who had created a new faster, stronger vampire race, who was on a mission to destroy older vampires. Including Stefan, Katherine, and Damon himself.

Damon hadn't even been on the same continent when Stefan was killed. He'd come home in time for Stefan's funeral, in time to helplessly witness Elena's devastation. Damon rubbed at his chest with one hand, wincing at the memory of how Elena's pain had resonated through the magical bond between them, drawing him home. That pain was how he had known Stefan was dead. Nothing else could have hurt Elena so much.

Damon and Elena's bond was at the root of what had happened to Elena now. The Guardians had linked them to keep Damon under control. They'd rightly decided that if Damon and Elena were connected, it would prevent Damon from following his worst impulses. They'd spelled it out for him: If he fed on the unwilling, Elena would suffer. If he killed a human, Elena would die.

Fat raindrops were beginning to fall, the light brown earth of the riverbank turning a splotchy brown. Shoving his hands into his pockets, Damon spoke again, staring down at his brother's grave. "I didn't know," he said quietly.

All they had wanted, what had consumed him and Elena both, was vengeance. And they had succeeded. They had tracked Jack down and Damon had killed him, had avenged Stefan's death.

After Jack died, Elena had finally felt at peace about Stefan. She'd turned to Damon, and for the first time they could love each other, without feeling that they were betraying Stefan. Damon knew he didn't deserve her. Whatever soul he'd once had, it had been corrupted long ago. But Elena had wanted him anyway.

They'd had two glorious weeks traveling together, enraptured with each other. Then Elena had collapsed, writhing in pain, and Mylea, the cold-faced Guardian who had bound them, arrived.

Damon had assumed it was safe to kill Jack Daltry because Jack was a vampire. It was humans who were forbidden; monsters were fair game to Damon. He'd been a fool. Jack had made *himself* a vampire, used science to replicate the strength and ferocity of the vampire while getting rid of a vampire's traditional vulnerabilities to wood, fire, sunlight.

He had changed himself through mortal means. He had never died; his human life had never ended. Jack wasn't a real vampire, just an imitation. There wasn't a drop of magic in him. As far as the Guardians were concerned, Damon had broken their bargain. And now was paying the price.

Dying.

Damon had brought her back to Dalcrest. Something in him had made him sure that she would want to be here, among the people she loved.

They'd battled unkillable monsters, saved the world together. Part of him, maybe foolishly, hoped that, together, they could all help him save her.

But, now that they were here and nothing had changed, he was terrified that they couldn't. Maybe Elena was beyond their reach. Damon shuddered at the thought, hunching his shoulders against the pounding rain.

"Stefan," he whispered, looking at the rain-soaked dirt of his brother's grave, "what can I do?" He had tried forcing his blood down her throat—she wouldn't have wanted it, but better a vampire than *gone*—but when he'd finally succeeded in making her swallow, it had done nothing.

Rage rose in him, and thunder cracked overhead. Damon turned his face up toward the sky, streams of water running through his hair, soaking his clothes. "Mylea!" he shouted, his own voice sounding raw and broken beneath the steady pounding of the storm. "I surrender! Punish me, I don't care. Anything. Just tell me what to do!" He paused and held his breath, listening and watching for some sign that the Guardians were prepared to bargain. He could feel tears running down his face, a little warmer than the rain-drops. "Please," he whispered. "Save her."

There was no response, nothing but the sounds of the river and the rain. If the Guardian could hear him, she clearly didn't care.

## 2

**M**eredith smoothed her hand across Elena's forehead. It was cold and clammy, and there were dark circles beneath Elena's eyes, startling against her pale skin. Meredith couldn't pull her eyes away from Elena's sleeping face, hoping against hope that something would happen, that she would suddenly crinkle her face in the half-annoyed way she always did in the mornings.

Stiffening, Meredith stared. Had there been a flicker of motion beneath Elena's closed eyelids?

"Elena?" Meredith said, keeping her voice soft and calm. "Can you hear me?"

There was no response. Of course there wasn't. They'd been trying for days, first Damon in Paris and then, once he'd gotten Elena home, Meredith had tried to wake her every way she could think of.

In all that time, nothing had changed. Elena had lain as still and passive as a mannequin, with only a shallow, steady breathing to show that she still lived.

Damon had said that, before she fell into this coma, Elena had been in terrible pain. Meredith was glad she had missed that, glad that Elena wasn't suffering now. But this—this silent, pale creature—terrified Meredith. It couldn't be Elena. Not clever, quick Elena who had survived so much, who had been closer than a sister to Meredith since they were kids.

Meredith rose from her chair next to the big white bed, unable to bring herself to look at Elena anymore. Instead, she moved around the bedroom, efficiently tidying: books off the nightstand and back onto the shelves, shoes neatly straightened on the closet floor. She kept her eyes fixed on what she was doing. She was not going to think about the still figure in the bed.

Meredith's teeth gave a hollow throb, and she rubbed absently at her gums with one finger. She would need to slip out to the woods soon to feed, but she couldn't leave Elena alone.

Alone. Their ranks were dwindling. Stefan was dead. Elena was *dying*. Alaric, Bonnie, and Matt were all still on their way: Bonnie from her new home, Alaric from an academic conference, Matt from visiting his girlfriend, Jasmine's, parents. Who knew where Damon was? He had disappeared hours ago.

Meredith picked up a thin, silver-patterned scarf and folded it neatly. Elena had been wearing this the last time Meredith had seen her. "I finally know," she'd told Meredith, her face so full of joy it hurt to remember. "Stefan wants me to live. He wants me to be happy. I can love Damon now ... it's okay."

Meredith blinked hard, pushing her tears away. Elena had been wrong. Everything was far from okay.

Clutching the scarf, Meredith jerked open a drawer. As she was about to stuff it inside, her hands faltered at the sight of the maroon book inside. Who would have guessed that poised, grown-up Elena Gilbert kept a high school yearbook in the nightstand next to her bed?

Gingerly, she pulled the book out of the drawer and flipped through its pages. Junior year. Their last real yearbook, the one before everything changed. There had been two yearbooks for senior year. The first, the one from the senior year Meredith remembered, had a memorial page for Elena Gilbert and Sue Carson. The other, for the changed world the Guardians had created, showed nothing but teams, classes, and clubs. Neither felt true now. But there was only one version of their junior year.

Her own face, years younger, smiled up from a picture of Homecoming Court. Elena had been class Princess, of course. Junior dance committee. She, Elena, and Bonnie had quit debate team after about a month, but they were in the picture, grinning like goons. An action shot of Matt on the football field, his face set as he powered past a tackle. It all seemed so *normal.*

She turned to the back, and her own handwriting stood out at her.

*Elena,*

*What can I say? My best friend and sister, you're always there for me. But I'll remember the picnics up at Hot Springs, driving to the fraternity party at UVA, Matt and the guys crashing your birthday sleepover. All the times getting ready for a dance together—you, me, Bonnie, and Caroline—was even better than the dance itself.*

*Have a super-fabu time in Paris this summer, you lucky girl, and remember this! Only one more year till FREEDOM!!!*

*XOXO*

*Meredith*

Such an ordinary yearbook message, between two ordinary girls. Before Elena's parents had died. Before the Salvatore brothers had come to Fell's Church, and nothing had ever been ordinary again. Elena and Meredith hadn't gotten that freedom the message promised, the freedom to grow up and be normal, to determine their own destinies. Neither had Bonnie nor Matt, nor had the people they'd fallen in love with as they got older.

Instead, they'd all been dragged under by the supernatural: vampires and werewolves, demons and Guardians. The responsibilities of saving everyone, of standing guard between everyday life and the darkness outside had pulled them all in, held them hostage.

*Elena most of all,* Meredith thought, and snuck a look back at the bed. Elena's chest moved almost imperceptibly as she breathed, her rattling, slow breaths loud in the quiet room. Elena had never really had a chance, not once she'd fallen for Stefan Salvatore.

The bedroom door creaked open, and Damon came in, silent and graceful. He looked to the bed first, a quick, worried glance, and then leaned against the doorjamb as if he was suddenly too tired to stand. His eyes, red-rimmed, met Meredith's, and she wondered if he'd been crying. Damon might rage or let himself be consumed with bitterness, but he never cried.

But maybe now, at the end of everything, he did.

\* \* \*

Matt parked crookedly, one wheel up on the curb, and bolted out of the car, slamming the door behind him. "I knew this would happen someday," he gritted out, teeth clenched, as he stormed down the sidewalk toward Elena's apartment building. "I knew Stefan and Damon would get her killed."

Jasmine followed more slowly, her golden-brown eyes serious. "Don't say that," she told him, laying a hand on his arm as they waited for the elevator. "Elena's not dead. We can't give up on her."

Matt bit his lip and stayed silent for the elevator ride up to Elena's apartment. The hall was quiet, and he hesitated a moment before knocking heavily on the apartment door.

"Take the worst possible thing you can imagine," he muttered, his voice hoarse with rage, "and that's it, that's the truth. Always." Beside him, Jasmine sucked in a breath and raised a hand to touch him again, just as the door swung open.

Damon was in the doorway, his pale face pinched, his dark hair messy. He looked more human than Matt had ever seen him. Before anyone could speak, Matt balled up his fist and punched Damon in the face as hard as he could.

Damon's head rocked back slightly and he blinked in surprise, a red mark on his white cheek.

"Didn't think you had it in you," he said with a thin, joyless smile. He touched his cheek lightly, and then let his hand drop, the smile disappearing. "I probably deserved that."

"Yeah, I figured," Matt said, shouldering past him into the apartment.

He stopped in the doorway of Elena's bedroom. His heart sank at the sight of her.

When he was little, there had been an amusement park up on Route 40 that had a fairytale theme to it. Matt's dad used to take him up there on Saturdays sometimes. He hadn't thought of it for years. But now it came rushing back. Silent and still, Elena reminded him of the Sleeping Beauty in the Hall of Fairies. The blonde princess, laid out like a sacrifice, not even a hint of movement. Pale and pretty and never changing.

Matt had always thought she'd looked dead.

Jasmine moved past him into the bedroom and felt Elena's throat for a pulse, then lifted one eyelid to look at her pupils. She bit her lip and looked back toward Matt. He could read the regret in her face.

"The doctors in Paris were baffled," Damon said from behind him. "They'd never seen anything like this. I tried the hospital there before booking a plane home, just in case. But it was useless."

"Yeah, that makes sense," Matt said. His mouth felt too dry, and his words sounded thick to his own ears. "The Guardians wouldn't mess around with any kind of human illness. If they gave this to her, they're the only ones who can fix it. We just need to make them do it."

Even as he said it, a cold rush of hopelessness spread through him. What did *they* have to offer the Guardians? What could possibly entice those clear-eyed, emotionless judges to give back Elena?

## 3

"Well, how did you get the Guardians to come when Elena made the original bargain with them?" Meredith asked. "Maybe we can convince them ..." Her voice trailed off, as she clearly tried and failed to imagine the Guardians of the Celestial Court being moved by anything they had to say. They had only listened to Elena because she was valuable to them.

Damon gritted his teeth and tried to keep his temper. They were wasting time, he was sure of it. The Celestial Guardians had no interest in helping them.

"The little Guardian, Andrés, went into a trance and told them Elena was ready to kill me," he said flatly. "That brought Mylea fast enough. Unfortunately, we've got a shortage of Earthly Guardians around here now."

"They saved you. Funny, isn't it, how everyone dies except you, Damon?" Matt said, glaring at him with blood-shot eyes. "Andrés. Stefan. And now—" His words broke off, and his mouth closed in a thin, miserable line.

A hot ball of hate burned in Damon's chest, and he momentarily imagined breaking Matt's neck. He could easily envision the shocked expression in the boy's blue eyes, the crisp snap of his spine. Then his shoulders slumped as he let the anger drain out of him. He deserved Matt's scorn. Everything Matt had said was true. The thing Damon was best at was survival, and now he'd outlived everyone—almost—who'd ever managed, despite everything, to love him. If Elena died, there would be no one.

He didn't want to think about it.

As footsteps approached the apartment door, he straightened, then rose from his seat. He thought he recognized the quick, light steps pattering down the hall, and the steady, heavier tread that followed. The door opened, and Bonnie burst in.

"We got here as fast as we could," she said rapidly. "The airport was a zoo, and then the traffic coming down from Richmond was—" She broke off. "Oh, *Meredith*." She flung herself across the room and into the taller girl's arms.

They clung to each other for a minute, Bonnie's face buried in Meredith's shoulder, and then she raised her head and held it high, sticking out her chin bravely. "So,

I'm gone for a couple of weeks and everything falls apart?" she said. Tears glimmered in her eyes, but her tone was casual, even joking.

*Good girl.* Damon knew the little redbird would stay brave, even though she was as scared as they all were.

Zander was leaning in the doorway, watching them all patiently. His longish white-blond hair fell over his forehead, and his eyes were solemn.

Letting go of Meredith, Bonnie took a deep breath. "So, what can I do?"

"Well," Meredith said, "we think you're probably our best chance of getting in touch with Mylea or the other Celestial Guardians. If you can go into a trance and reach them, maybe we can convince them to save Elena."

Bonnie grimaced. "I've been trying," she said. "Ever since you called me. But … nothing. If they can hear me, they're not responding."

"It's not going to work," Damon said, unable to stop himself. Why would the Guardians listen to them? If they were letting this happen to Elena, the Guardians had written her and her Powers off. They'd never had the slightest interest in the rest of them, other than planning to kill Damon himself.

"You have a better idea?" Matt sneered.

"Try to contact Elena instead," Damon said quickly, the idea coming to him as he spoke. "You did it when Klaus had her, and we didn't have anything, not even a body then. Now we've still got Elena, she's just … We can't reach her." His chest felt uncomfortably tight as he finished the sentence.

Whatever Bonnie heard in his voice, her face softened. "I'll try," she said and made her way to where Elena laid.

The way Elena's hands were folded across her chest was too much like a corpse, and Damon grimaced.

"Oh, *Elena*," Bonnie said, her brown eyes shining with tears. Standing at the bedside, she touched Elena's forehead gently, just for a moment.

The others trailed in after her. Jasmine and Matt stood on the other side of the bed, Matt only glancing at Elena briefly before fixing his gaze on the wall. Jasmine took his hand and squeezed it hard. Zander leaned against the wall, holding a bag of Bonnie's supplies, while Meredith hovered at the foot of the bed, her fingers twisting nervously. Damon stood in the doorway.

Bonnie took Elena's limp hands in hers and shut her eyes, her forehead crinkling in concentration. Then she opened her eyes again and shook her head, letting go of Elena. "I'm going to need to focus," she said. "Can you guys wait outside?"

Damon stepped farther into the room, crossing his arms across his chest. "I'm staying."

Bonnie sighed. "Is it any use arguing with you about this?" she asked. When Damon stayed silent, she gave him a rueful half smile. "Then I won't bother. But everybody else out. I need quiet."

Matt looked like he wanted to object, but he filed out with the others. As Zander left, he handed the bag he was holding to Bonnie, brushing his fingers against hers as he passed it over.

"Okay," Bonnie said, businesslike, when the others were all gone and the door was closed behind them. "If you want to stay, you have to help." She handed him the bag. "Pull out the purple and blue candles, and put them on the nightstand near her head. They're good for deep healing. I don't know if they'll help, but they can't hurt."

Damon followed her directions. He kept his eyes fixed on the candles as he arranged and lit them.

Once the candles were in place, Bonnie took out a bronze bowl and set it on the padded bench at the foot of Elena's bed. Pulling out an assortment of little bags, she started adding pinches of dried herbs to the bowl. "Anise for dreams," she told Damon absently, and tipped in some limp dry flower petals. "Chrysanthemum petals for healing and protection. Mugwort, that's for psychic powers and traveling. I just have to reach her." She added a splash of oil from a small bottle, then pulled out a silver lighter and, with a flick of her finger, set fire to the small pile of herbs in the bowl. They smoldered slowly, a trickle of black smoke rising up toward the ceiling.

"Since when do you need anything to light a flame, redbird?" Damon asked, and Bonnie tilted her chin in acknowledgment of his point.

"I figure I should save my energy," she said, and dug a thin silver dagger out of the bag. "Cut me a piece of Elena's hair, please."

Damon hesitated before moving back to the head of the bed. Elena's mouth was relaxed, a tiny bit open, and her thick golden lashes brushed her cheekbones. Thin, bluish capillaries ran across her eyelids, and her brow was smooth, untroubled. She looked like a doll or an empty image. As if there were no Elena left in there at all.

Her hair slid silkily across his fingers as he lifted a lock, and he could smell the citrus scent of her shampoo. Cutting through the hair, he winced as he accidentally pulled it tight, but Elena didn't react.

"Okay," Bonnie said, taking the lock of hair from him and dropping it into the bowl. The sickening smell of burning hair filled the room. "Now, cut her arm."

Damon's gaze shot up to meet hers. Bonnie looked at him squarely, her mouth set. "We need her blood," she said.

*Of course. It always has to be blood.* If anyone ought to know that, it was a vampire. Blood and hair, intimate and primal, would lead Bonnie to Elena if anything would. He lifted Elena's arm, and Bonnie slid the bowl beneath it as Damon used the silver knife to make a thin, shallow scratch on the underside of Elena's forearm. He half hoped for a twitch of pain as he cut, but again, Elena didn't react. A few drops of blood dripped into the bowl before Bonnie pulled it away. There was a soft, sizzling noise.

Damon could smell the richness of Elena's blood, and his canines ached and sharpened in response, but he barely noticed. Taking a tissue from the box by the bed, he pressed it against the spreading red line on Elena's arm for a few moments until the bleeding had stopped.

"Now what?" he began to say, but his voice died as he turned back to Bonnie. A sensation of Power rose and filled the room, making Damon's skin tingle. Bonnie had already slipped into a trance, her eyes wide and blank. Her pupils dilated as she stared down into the flames in the brass bowl.

Her hands rested lightly on the end of Elena's bed. Her breathing slowed and deepened. As Damon watched, Bonnie's eyes flickered, tracking something that only she could see.

Crossing the room, Damon let himself lounge against the windowsill, gazing out. Bonnie could be in a trance for a very long time. Outside the window, it was still pitch-black, although it must be the early hours of the morning by now. He unloosed a questioning tendril of his own Power, searching into the darkness.

There wasn't much out there. The sharp, predatory mind of an owl swooping silently through the sky. A wily fox slipped through the bushes near the apartment building. Farther away, he could sense the quiet consciousness of the humans asleep through the town.

Behind him, Bonnie's mind was questing, gently but determined. He could feel the others, too, each one's mind churning restlessly as they waited outside the bedroom.

But, even though she was right behind him, lying in that white-draped bed, he could feel nothing of Elena. Damon felt as if something inside him had been ripped apart. His Elena, just one last breath away from leaving him forever.

And then he thought he saw one slender golden eyebrow twitch, just a millimeter.

"Bonnie," he said, his throat constricting. But the little witch, deep in her trance, didn't hear him. He came closer to the bed again, close enough that he could feel the heat of the candles burning all around Elena.

Nothing. She could have been a statue. He sent his Power out desperately, but there was no glimmer of consciousness from her.

He must have imagined it.

Damon crouched down and brought his face closer to Elena's, watching her carefully. Time passed and he stayed still, his gaze intent on Elena's face. He was a predator; he could keep his mind clear and his eyes sharp for hours. But there was nothing.

He couldn't leave here, not while there was still that cruel drop of hope. But if Elena died, then it would be time to take off the ring that had let him walk in sunlight all these years. He could step into the sun and let go at last.

His jaw tightened. He wasn't going to give up yet. After all, Elena had survived so much before this.

Dawn was breaking, sending long swathes of pink and gold across the sky, by the time Bonnie finally stirred. She blinked at Damon, seemingly confused. There were dark shadows under her eyes, and her usually creamy skin looked pale and wan.

"Oh," she said, her voice small. "Oh, Damon." She pressed one slim hand against her mouth, as if holding back her own words.

Damon straightened, feeling as if he were stepping in front of the firing line. Maybe, just maybe, he was wrong. The tiny spark of hope in his chest flickered and began to burn again. "Well?" he asked.

Bonnie's eyes reddened, then overflowed, tears tracking down her cheeks. "I don't know," she said, shaking her head. "I can't even begin to tell what's wrong. I couldn't reach her. It was like—like she's already gone."

Damon jerked backward, and Bonnie reached out a trembling hand toward him. "I think," she sobbed, "I think it might be time to start saying good-bye. Whatever the Celestial Guardians did to her, I don't think Elena's coming back."

"*No.*" Damon heard his own voice, sharp as a whipcrack, and he strode forward, straight past Bonnie, and flung open the bedroom door. The others were out there, all of them, but he ignored their babble of questions as he shouldered past them. He had a brief impression of Meredith's face, anxious and strained, before he left the apartment.

He didn't know where he was going. But there had to be *something* Damon could do, *somewhere* he could go to help Elena. He'd lost everyone. Everyone he'd ever truly cared for was dead. He wasn't going to say good-bye to Elena—not now, not ever. He wasn't going to lose her.

## 4

"I love you, Damon," Elena whispered.

He couldn't hear her. None of them could hear her. Most of the time she couldn't hear them, either, just enough to get the fleeting impression of tears and whispers and arguments. She couldn't understand more than a word or two, sometimes just enough to recognize a voice.

She thought she'd heard Damon. But she had to admit there was the possibility she'd imagined it, that she was imagining all the familiar distant voices, just to keep herself company.

She was dying. She must be. There had been that terrible pain, Mylea had appeared, and then Elena had found herself in this place of emptiness.

Elena had hoped for a while that she might find Stefan. She'd seen his ghost, she knew his consciousness still lingered somewhere, but the place she was in now didn't feel like any kind of spectral realm. She'd given up looking for Stefan when it became clear that there was no one here except Elena.

A soft gray light shone all around her, just enough to illuminate what seemed like a fog. It felt like a fog, too. She was surrounded by a damp chill.

She'd walked for miles, but nothing changed. She might not have believed she was moving at all, except for the ache in her feet. When she stopped and stood still, the fog was just the same.

Elena clenched her fists and glared into the gray nothingness. She wasn't going to let this happen. She wasn't going to lie down and die, just because the Celestial Guardians wanted her to.

"Hey!" she shouted. "Hey! I'm still here!" Her words sounded muffled to her own ears, as if she was wrapped in a thick layer of cotton. "Let me out!" she shouted, trying to get louder, fiercer. Somebody had to be in charge here, and she would get their attention and *make* them let her go.

Elena's stomach jolted nervously. What if no one ever responded? She couldn't stay here forever. The moment she thought this, finally, something changed. The fog drew back, and a sunlit road appeared.

Elena recognized the street. If she ignored the banks of gray nothingness on either side, it was the road that led to the house she had grown up in, back in Fell's Church. She recognized a long crack in the asphalt, the short grass growing at the edge of the road. But she hadn't lived there for years, not since that final year of high school. Stefan had bought it for her before he died, but she had been able to bring herself to visit only once.

Elena had a sudden, almost physical longing to walk down the path, to feel the sunlight on her shoulders, smell the summer scent of just-cut grass. As she watched, the sunshine intensified at the far end of the road, glowing so brightly Elena had to squint.

It was pulling her toward it, a steady, warm tug somewhere in the middle of her chest. There was peace down that road, she knew.

*No.* She stepped back, away from the road. They weren't going to trap her so easily.

"*Walk into the light?*" she shouted, suddenly furious. "You've got to be kidding!"

The longing only increased. At the end of that road, she was sure, was almost everything she had ever wanted. Stefan, alive again, his leaf-green eyes shining with excitement at seeing her. Her parents, just as young and happy as they'd been when they died. Elena could almost see their welcoming faces, and it made her ache with love and loneliness.

Unwillingly, she raised a foot, ready to step forward, and then forced herself still.

"No," she said, her voice cracking. She swallowed hard and steadied it, then spoke again more firmly. "*No*. I refuse. I am Elena Gilbert, and I am a Guardian. I still have a part to play in the living world. Send me back."

The road stretched farther in front of her, sunlit and tempting. Grinding her teeth, Elena swung around and turned her back on it.

When she turned, she could see the same formless fog. But now there was a dark shape moving through it. *A person*, Elena realized. Her heart began to pound harder, and her mouth went dry. Was it someone coming in response to her call? For a panicky moment, she imagined a Grim Reaper, silent in black, come to collect her.

But no. As the figure came closer, Elena was able to make out that it was Mylea, the Celestial Guardian who had been overseeing Elena's life for years. When she finally halted in front of Elena, Mylea looked as serene and unruffled as ever, her golden hair pulled back into a bun, her ice-blue gaze level and cool.

"Elena, you made a bargain," she said firmly. "Damon killed a human, and so you have to die. You agreed to this, years ago."

"That's not fair," Elena said, scowling. She sounded like a child, she realized, and she made an effort to temper her voice so that she sounded more reasonable. "Damon was working under the assumption that Jack Daltry was a vampire, and so he could be killed without breaking our agreement. Jack *was* a vampire. He drank blood, and he had all the strengths of a vampire. He was a monster."

Mylea sighed. "As I've already explained to you, the fact that Jack Daltry chose to use his scientific gifts to mutilate himself did not make him less human." Her face softened, just a fraction. "He might have been a monster, but he was a human one."

"But we didn't *know* that," Elena told her, exasperated.

"You knew that he had never died, that he had never gone through the transformations every vampire suffers through. You knew that he and his creations did not have the flaws that weaken true vampires." Mylea spread her hands. "If anyone should have been able to recognize a true vampire, it would be you and Damon Salvatore."

"Jack was dangerous," Elena snapped. "The Guardians ought to be *thanking* us. I'm supposed to protect people."

Mylea shrugged, a graceful tilt of her shoulders. "You were warned that he was not your concern."

It was true; the Guardians had warned her. But in such a roundabout way that she'd had no idea of the possible consequences of hunting Jack. Fear ran through Elena, and she swallowed hard. This was real. She hadn't quite believed that the Guardians would kill her, but it was true. They would let her die.

"Please," she said impulsively, reaching out for Mylea's arm. "There must be something I can do. Isn't there any way to change this? I've served the Guardians for a long time."

Mylea's expression remained as emotionless as ever, but Elena thought she saw a flash of sympathy deep in her eyes.

"There must be *something*," Elena said desperately.

Mylea frowned, a tiny crease appearing between her slim eyebrows. "There is one way you can change your future," she admitted.

"Please," Elena begged again. "Anything."

"If you can go back and change the course of things, prove that you and the Salvatore brothers can live without destroying one another or other people, you can have your life back." Mylea tilted her head a little, watching Elena closely. Obviously, she thought that she had made herself clear.

"What do you mean?" Elena asked, startled. *Destroying one another? They* loved *one another.*

Mylea shook her head. "You and the Salvatore brothers have been in a dangerous cycle for years. *You* were the one who brought them back together after they'd been apart for centuries, Elena, and their rivalry over you led to every-thing that's gone wrong here since then. The destruction of Fell's Church was a direct effect of your relationship."

Elena gasped, stricken.

Eyes narrowing, Mylea went on. "The vampire Katherine's jealousy over both Salvatore brothers' obses-sion with you led to the beginnings of death and violence in Fell's Church. Her death as a result of her actions there led to the vampire Klaus's attacks on the town. Damon Salvatore's rage over your choosing his brother over him resulted in the kitsune demons gaining a foothold there and destroying Fell's Church at last."

"But the Guardians brought Fell's Church back," Elena objected.

"And yet the death continued," Mylea told her. "The students at Dalcrest College, Klaus's victims, the Guardian Andrés—all had their roots in the damaged love between the three of you. Everything has consequences, Elena."

Elena pressed a hand to her forehead, feeling dizzy and sickened. It wasn't true, was it? She and Damon and Stefan were responsible for all the horror that had surrounded them. "What do you mean 'go back'?"

"I can send you back to when it all began," Mylea said. Her eyes, a lighter blue than Elena's own, held Elena's gaze. "William Tanner's death was the first time Damon Salvatore had killed in years, and it was the first link in the chain of violence. If you can prevent it from happening and keep Damon from giving in to the darkness within him, perhaps you can turn the course of events that will, in the present timeline, eventually kill you all."

"Damon hadn't killed for years?" Elena said slowly. She hadn't known that. Neither had Stefan, she was sure of it.

She'd thought her love had *saved* him. Had saved both Damon and Stefan. *The Guardians twist the truth*, she reminded herself, and swallowed hard, pushing away the tears that prickled at the back of her eyes. She wanted to argue with Mylea, but instead she asked, "You can send me back in time?"

Mylea nodded briskly. "You'll be back in your old body, in your old life," she said. "This is an opportunity to relive those days and change things." Her eyes seemed to soften slightly, and she went on, "Don't take this challenge lightly, Elena. What you change in the past will affect your future. Once you return, everything will be different. You might not be able to be with either of the Salvatore brothers."

The gray mist seemed to swirl before Elena's eyes. She could lose Damon, too? But their love was strong, she reminded herself. Even when she had been determined to only love Stefan, fate had pulled her and Damon together.

"I'll do it," she said, trying to feel confident. She didn't know what she could do, not yet, but she would stop Damon from killing, somehow fix the hatred between the brothers before it could blossom into something that would affect more than the two of them. "But how?"

Mylea's lips quirked up in an almost tender smile. "Love is a very powerful force," she said quietly, and raised one hand to press against Elena's forehead. Elena had a moment to feel the cool strength of that slender hand, and then everything faded to black.

## 5

Dear Diary,
    I can't believe it.
    Here I am in my old home at 5:30 in the morning, just a few hours before my senior year of high school begins.
    Again.

I remember this morning vividly, the last morning of my life before I met Stefan Salvatore. The Elena I was then—the one who should be here now—was so lost. I didn't feel like I belonged here, or like I belonged anywhere. I was searching for something that was just out of reach.

My bedroom looks just the way it always did, warm and cozy. My bay window gives me a view onto the quince tree outside. Down the hall are dear Aunt Judith and my darling baby *sister, Margaret, who's only four and tucked up tight in bed, not half-grown and miles away.*

*Everything feels as if I might break it, it's so fragile. This moment has been gone for years.*

Elena stopped writing and stared at her last line, shaking her head. Soon, she'd see everyone, everything, unchanged. They'd been so naïve—in a good way—focused on popularity and high school romances, and unaware of the darkness that hovered just outside their pleasant lives. She'd never appreciated what she had then. This time, she'd know to savor those moments of innocence.

But she wasn't just here to revisit her past.

Tapping her pen against the pages of the small book with the blue velvet cover, she thought for a moment, and then bent her head and began writing again.

*Stefan is* alive *here. When I think about being with him, my hands start to shake and I can hardly breathe. Part of me died with him, and now I'm going to see him again. Whatever happens next, at least I'll have that.*

*If I'm going to save Damon, stop the destruction Mylea outlined, I can't be with Stefan this time. It hurts. It hurts a lot. But if I want Damon to listen to me, I have to be with him, not Stefan. I already know how things turn out if I pursue Stefan now.*

*I love them both. So much. I always have.*

*But I've learned my lesson about trying to have them both. If I want them both in my life, things fall apart. They always fall apart, no matter what we do. I have to choose. And, if I can keep Damon from killing Mr. Tanner, maybe I can save us all.*

With a click and a buzz, Elena's alarm clock went off. Closing her journal, she got up. Soon, it would be time to go to school. Would she remember enough about who she had been then? She worried that somehow, everyone would see that she was the wrong Elena, in the wrong time.

*A hot bath and some coffee, and I'll calm down,* she thought. She had time.

After a leisurely bath, she took her time getting dressed. The clothes—all the gorgeous new outfits she'd gotten in Paris—looked outdated to her now, but she still sort of loved them. She remembered what she'd worn on this day, the first day of her senior year. A pale rose top and white linen shorts. She pulled them on again. They made her look tempting, as sweet and refreshing as a raspberry sundae, she thought as she looked critically into the mirror, pulling back her hair with a deep rose ribbon.

"Elena! You're going to be late for school!" Aunt Judith's voice drifted up from below. Glancing in the mirror one last time—her face was a trifle grim, as if she were headed into battle, but that couldn't be helped—Elena grabbed her backpack and headed for the stairs.

Downstairs, Aunt Judith was burning something on the stove, and Margaret was eating cereal at the kitchen table. The sight of them stopped Elena in her tracks for a second. She'd forgotten how little Margaret was then. And Aunt Judith had still been wearing her flyaway hair long.

Elena pushed herself back into motion and kissed Aunt Judith quickly on the cheek. "Good morning," she said lightly. "Sorry, I don't have time for breakfast."

"But, Elena, you can't just go off without eating. You need your protein—"

It was all coming back to her. She felt like an actress, mouthing familiar lines she'd said a hundred times before. "I'll get a doughnut before school," she said, dropping a kiss on the top of Margaret's silky head and turning to go.

"But, Elena—"

"Don't worry, Aunt Judith," Elena said cheerfully. "It'll all be fine." At the front door, she spun to take one last quick look at them. Margaret, still half-asleep, licked her spoon. Aunt Judith, her eyes full of love, gave Elena a small, worried smile.

Elena's heart ached a little. Part of her wanted to go back, forget school and the future, and sit down at the table with them. So much had happened since this moment, and she'd never believed she would be back here like this again. But she couldn't stay. Margaret wiggled her fingers in a wave, and Elena, spurring herself into movement, winked at the little girl as she went through the door.

"Elena," Aunt Judith said. "I really think—"

She closed the door behind her, cutting off Aunt Judith's protests, and stepped out onto the front porch.

And stopped.

The world outside was silent, the street deserted. The tall, pretty Victorian houses seemed to loom above her. Overhead, the sky was milky and opaque, and the air felt oppressively heavy.

It was as if the whole street were holding its breath, waiting for something to happen.

Out of the corner of her eye, Elena saw something move. Something was watching her.

She turned and caught sight of a huge black crow, the biggest crow she had ever seen, sitting in the quince tree in her front yard. It was completely still, and its glittering black eyes were fixed on her with an intent, almost human gaze.

Elena bit back a laugh and turned away, letting her eyes slide over the crow as if she hadn't noticed it.

*Damon.* She had almost forgotten that this was the first time she'd seen him, that he'd watched her— frightened her—as a crow this first morning. There was a glad little bubble of joy rising in her chest, but she suppressed the urge to call out to him. It wasn't the time, not yet.

Instead, she took a deep breath, hopped off the porch, and strode confidently down the street. Behind her, she heard a harsh croak and the flapping of wings, and she smiled to herself. Damon couldn't stand being ignored. She didn't turn back around.

It was only a few blocks to the high school, and Elena spent the walk reminiscing. There was the coffee shop she and Matt had gone to on their first date junior year; there was the little health food shop where Aunt Judith had insisted on buying her special organic cereal. There was the house of the terrible Kline twins, who Elena had babysat during her sophomore year of school.

In her real life, it hadn't been that long since Elena had been to Fell's Church, but things had changed since she was in high school. Stores had closed and opened, houses were remodeled. This was the way it had been when she'd lived here, the way it was supposed to be.

At the school, a crowd of her friends had gathered in the parking lot, chattering and showing off their new clothes. It was everyone who mattered, plus four or five girls who had hung around them in the hopes of gathering some scraps of popularity.

Elena winced. *Everyone who mattered.* The nasty thought had slotted right into her mind. The Elena who belonged here had thought that.

One by one, her best friends hugged her in welcome. They looked so *young,* Elena thought, her heart aching. They all thought they were so sophisticated, but their seventeen- and eighteen-year-old faces still had childish curves, and their eyes were wide with thinly veiled excitement at the first day of their senior year.

Caroline, her green eyes narrow, laid one cool cheek against Elena's for a second and then stepped back. "Welcome home, Elena," she said dryly. "It must feel like the backwoods for you after Paris."

Her expression was stiff and resentful, and Elena wondered at how she had managed to not notice then how much the other girl hated her.

Elena shrugged and laughed a little, feeling awkward. "Paris was nice, but there's no place like home."

For a moment, she tried to focus in on Caroline, to read her aura, but it was hopeless. Elena wasn't a Guardian here, and so she didn't have those powers anymore. It was a strange, helpless feeling to lose them.

Then Bonnie flung her arms around Elena, her red curls tickling the taller girl's chin, and Elena relaxed.

"Do you like my hair? I think it makes me look taller." Bonnie fluffed up her bangs and smiled.

"Gorgeous," Elena said, laughing. "But maybe not tall."

Once Bonnie let go, Meredith moved forward for a warm hug. Raising one elegant eyebrow, she considered Elena. "Well, your hair is two shades lighter from the sun ... but where's your tan? I thought you were living it up on the French Riviera."

Wait. Elena remembered this. She lifted her own pale hands and said, "You know I never tan."

"Just a minute, that reminds me!" Bonnie grabbed one of Elena's hands. "Guess what I learned from my cousin this summer? Palm reading!"

There were a few groans, and someone laughed. Elena's breath rushed out of her. Of course; she had almost forgotten. This was the first time Bonnie had shown her Power. She'd seen the future in Elena's palm. Slowly, Elena flattened out her hand, opening it to Bonnie's gaze.

"Laugh while you can," Bonnie said serenely, peering into Elena's palm. "My cousin told me I'm psychic."

There was something Elena had said then, the first time this happened, but she couldn't remember exactly what. It didn't matter anyway. What had mattered here was what Bonnie had seen in her hand: Stefan.

"Okay," Bonnie said, frowning as she traced the lines on Elena's palm with one finger. "Now, this is your life line—or is it your heart line?" In the crowd around them, someone snickered. "Quiet. I'm reaching into the void.

I see … I see …" Bonnie frowned. "I don't get this. It says you have two loves, Elena."

Elena's chest tightened. This wasn't right.

Bonnie touched one end of the line running across the center of Elena's palm. The line forked there, splitting into two lines wrapping around the side of Elena's hand. "See? Your heart line divides into two."

"Greedy," Caroline said, not quite jokingly.

Elena blinked, bewildered. Bonnie should have started talking about Stefan. She was supposed to say he was dark and handsome, and he had been tall once. But instead Bonnie must be seeing something of what had happened in the time after this, the truths of Elena herself, the one who didn't belong here.

"I can see the two loves," Bonnie went on. "But there's something else here. …" Her eyes widened, and, with a quick, sudden movement, she dropped Elena's hand as if it had burned her.

"What's wrong?" Elena asked, suddenly frightened. She reached out to her, but Bonnie backed away, tucking her own hands behind her back.

"It's nothing," she said. "Palm reading's silly anyway."

Elena was having trouble catching her breath. Bonnie's Power was incredibly strong, although in this time she didn't know how to use it. If there was something in Elena's future that frightened Bonnie this badly, then

Elena should be frightened, too. "Bonnie?" Elena asked anxiously, reaching toward her again. "*Tell* me."

There was something panicked in the smaller girl's face, and she shook her head. "I don't want to talk about it anymore. It's a dumb game."

Unsure of what to do, Elena wavered. She couldn't *make* Bonnie tell her anything. But if what Bonnie saw in her palm had changed, maybe it was a clue to how her plan was going to work, how things would turn out differently. It might be important.

But maybe it was just showing all the awful things that had already happened to Elena after this moment—the future that hadn't yet appeared for Elena of the past. The future she was going to change.

Elena swallowed hard. That was it, it must be, she reassured herself. Bonnie was seeing things she didn't understand, frightening things. But it wasn't Elena's future, not now.

"We should head into class," Meredith said, sounding slightly irritated as she glanced at her watch.

They were turning toward the school building when the roar of a finely tuned motor stopped them in their tracks. The group of girls swung around to look.

"Well, now," Caroline said, her green eyes speculative. "Quite a car."

"Quite a Porsche," Meredith corrected dryly.

Elena didn't look; she kept her gaze firmly fixed on the brick façade of the school. But she could hear it, the purring of the sleek black Porsche's engine as its driver searched for a spot, and her heart pounded wildly in her chest.

A new student had arrived, one she'd been waiting for despite herself.

*Stefan.*

lena's heart clenched. She *had* to look. She couldn't help herself.

Talking to Stefan, touching Stefan, wasn't an option. But she was going to take this chance to at least see him, a chance she had thought would never come again.

The purr of the engine died, and she heard the car door open before she glanced up.

"Oh my God," Caroline whispered.

"You can say that again," breathed Bonnie.

Oh, *Stefan*.

He was alive. He was *here*. He looked just as he had that last night they'd been together. Elena wanted to run to him and wrap herself around his lean body, run her fingers through his wavy dark hair, kiss the sad curve of his mouth. Sunglasses shielded his face like a mask, but

Elena knew Stefan well enough to see through the protection they provided. She could sense the misery that had driven him to enroll in school, had made him try to act like a teenage boy so that he could have some brief human contact.

Everything in her pulled toward him. But if she ran to him, everything would lead straight to where she had come from. Stefan dead, Elena dying, Damon broken.

Elena bit her lip so hard she tasted blood, and stayed where she was.

"Who *is* that masked man?" Meredith asked, and everyone giggled.

"Do you see that jacket?" one of the hangers-on asked. "That's Italian, as in *Roma*."

"How would you know? You've never been farther than Rome, New York, in your life!" her friend answered.

Stefan was heading toward the school, a few rows of cars between him and the group of girls. The rhythm of his steps hitched and paused for just a moment. Elena felt a jolt. He had caught sight of her, she knew. There was a moment when he just stared from behind his sunglasses, his gaze burning into Elena. What was he seeing, she wondered? Her uncanny resemblance to Katherine, certainly, but Elena couldn't help hoping there was more to it than that. Even this early, could Stefan sense something more in her than the looks of his lost love?

After a moment, Stefan began to walk again, continuing smoothly on. Elena stared after him, feeling raw and exposed.

"Uh-oh," another hanger-on said, a touch of envy in her voice. "Elena's got that look again. The hunting look."

"New Boy had better be careful."

Elena pulled herself together and slapped on an expression of disdain. Tossing her head, she began to walk toward the school. "Hardly," she said. "I've got big plans for this year. And they don't include some random boy, no matter how nice his car is."

The other girls crowded behind her in a close-knit pack.

"What kind of plans?"

"Surely you can fit in Mr. Cute-Dark-and-Mysterious."

Without replying, Elena led them through the front door of the school. A long corridor stretched before them, and Stefan's lean figure was disappearing through the office doorway just ahead. Some of the other girls were already drifting toward the office window, eagerly craning their necks. "Nice rear view," someone said, giggling. Caroline was with them, but she wasn't looking through the window at Stefan. Instead, she was watching Elena speculatively.

Deliberately, Elena avoided her gaze. "Do you have my schedule?" she asked Meredith.

"Sure," Meredith said after a pause, handing it to her. Elena remembered that her friend had picked it up for her when Elena had skipped orientation. "We've got trig on the second floor in five minutes."

A few of the girls who had been watching Stefan had turned away from the windows now, discouraged by Elena's lack of interest. *Good*, Elena thought. She couldn't have him, she knew, but somehow she didn't want anyone else going after him.

"Let's go," she said to Meredith.

Meredith and Bonnie exchanged a look, and Meredith followed Elena upstairs. Just as they reached the classroom, Meredith laid a cool hand on Elena's arm, stopping her.

"Did something happen in France?" she asked quietly.

Elena frowned. "What do you mean?"

"Nothing," Meredith said slowly, her calm gray eyes scanning over Elena. "You just seem different, that's all. Distracted."

A semi-hysterical giggle rose up in Elena's chest—*Well, you see, Meredith, I've been sent back from the future to stop one of the vampires I'm in love with from killing someone, or I'll die*—and she choked it back and smiled at Meredith instead. "I'm fine."

All through trig, Elena shut out the teacher's droning voice, taking the textbook that was handed to her without glancing at it. She knew for a *fact* that she was never again going to use trigonometry. Tapping her fingers idly against her desk, she tried to plan instead.

She needed to meet Damon. But how? The first time they'd met, it had been partly because she looked like Katherine, but *mostly* because she was with Stefan, and the Damon she'd met then would be damned if he let his baby brother have her. But she couldn't wrap herself around Stefan and wait for Damon to come.

If Damon accepted that he was the one she wanted, if she could get him to love her now the way he would in the future, she could keep him from killing anyone. He wouldn't be so angry. He wouldn't be ready to strike out.

"Can anyone tell me what the sine function is?" the teacher asked, breaking in on Elena's thoughts. Mrs. Halpern's eyes swept over the class, and Elena instinctively hunched a little, avoiding the teacher's gaze.

Meredith began to answer the question. She was so beautiful, Elena thought, with her olive skin and heavy black lashes. More than that, Meredith looked happy. And *human*.

She'd had troubles in her life at this point already, Elena knew. A vampire had attacked her grandfather, stolen her brother. But this confident high school Meredith was barely aware of the horrors in her family's past. She was already moving on.

Here, in this classroom, Elena could see exactly how miserable Meredith was in the future Elena had come from. Elena had known, of course, that Meredith hated being a vampire. But Elena hadn't seen this contentment in years.

Elena sighed and thoughtfully curled a long, silky strand of hair around her finger. Could she fix Meredith, too, if she could keep Damon from killing Mr. Tanner? The road that had led to Meredith's transformation was a long and twisting one, but it had started here. If Meredith was kept clear of the supernatural, if she never suspected the dangers beginning to descend on Fell's Church, maybe she would leave. Go to an Ivy League college as she'd planned, have a successful, human life.

The rest of the morning passed in a blur. Stefan was in none of her early classes, thank God, although she knew she'd see him in history that afternoon. She couldn't stop herself from looking for him in the halls. She didn't see him, but she had a constant, exultant awareness that he was here—and *alive*.

She tried to make plans, but she was constantly distracted. Everyone wanted Elena's attention: Boys flirted with her; girls curried her favor with scraps of gossip. She had forgotten what it was like to be the queen of school. Matt *was* in one of her morning classes, and she met his smile with quiet panic. She didn't know what to do with Matt yet. Her friend was going to have to get his heart broken … again.

By lunchtime, she was sick of acting like she cared about the popularity, and she slipped down toward the cafeteria alone. Caroline was outside, posed casually against a wall in a model's slouch. The two boys she was talking to nudged each other as Elena came toward them.

Elena wanted to just walk on by. She remembered *this*, too, and all the awful things Caroline had done later. She had plotted to destroy Elena, for no reason, out of jealousy and pure spite.

But Caroline's chin was tilted up, and her eyes staring deliberately past Elena, as if the other girl was beneath her notice. Every line of her body broadcast pure hostility. Her hatred would only increase. If Elena didn't deal with her now, it was bound to be worse later.

"Hi," Elena said briefly to the boys. To Caroline she asked, "Want to get lunch?"

Caroline barely glanced at Elena as she pushed her glossy auburn hair back. "What, at the *royal table?*" she asked scathingly.

Elena suppressed an urge to roll her eyes and instead forced a smile. "Please come," she said gently. "I want to hear about your summer. I missed you." It was true, sort of. She'd known Caroline since kindergarten; they'd been good friends until this moment. Maybe she could change things here, too. Maybe this was a chance to fix everything she regretted.

Elena kept going into the cafeteria, not giving Caroline a chance to snap back an answer. Caroline followed but, a few steps in, her fingers fastened hard on Elena's arm. "A lot of things changed while you were gone this summer, Elena," she hissed warningly. "And just maybe your time on the throne is running out."

"You'd make a better queen than I do. Take it," Elena said agreeably, scanning the crowd as Caroline stood dumfounded. "Are you getting hot lunch?" It was a relief to see Meredith and Bonnie already sitting at their table. Caroline, temporarily silenced, followed as Elena got her lunch and went to join them.

"That new boy is in my biology class," Bonnie announced. "I sit right across from him. And his name is Stefan—Stefan Salvatore—and he's from Italy. He's boarding with old Mrs. Flowers on the edge of town. He picked up your books when you dropped them, didn't he, Caroline? Did he say anything?"

"Not much," said Caroline shortly. She was still watching Elena from the corner of her eyes, her forehead slightly creased.

"There he is," Meredith said, looking across the lunchroom.

Elena's head shot up. There Stefan was, hesitating at the door of the cafeteria, and then crossing it with long, smooth strides, heading for the hall that led toward the other side of the school. He wouldn't eat, of course. He had probably fed on the blood of a bird or small animal before school.

Stefan glanced toward their table, and Elena felt his eyes slide over her as viscerally as if he'd touched her. And then he passed by, his jaw tight. Elena swallowed and looked away.

Caroline was still watching him. She had the slightest hint of a smirk on her lovely face.

Caroline wanted Stefan, Elena knew. A few days after this, they'd started hanging out during lunch, had gone to Homecoming together. And then Elena and Stefan had come together, and he'd forgotten Caroline completely. No wonder she'd hated Elena more and more.

On an impulse, Elena nudged her. "You should talk to him," she said.

It was the last thing she wanted, really. But Caroline's fury over Elena taking Stefan had led to so much horror. And if Stefan was out of the way, in Caroline's orbit, it would be easier for Elena to focus on Damon.

Besides, Stefan would never love Caroline. He'd be perfectly safe with her.

Caroline flicked a glance at Elena. "Who says I want to talk to him?" she said cooly.

But a moment later, Caroline was staring at the door Stefan had gone through. Elena took a long drink of her water. She'd set something in motion.

It might be necessary, but that didn't mean she had to like it.

## 7

"Aunt Judith wants me home right after school today," Elena lied. "I have to hear all about Margaret's first day of nursery school, I guess." She was leaning against her locker, Matt looking down at her with his honest blue eyes. They ignored the people streaming past, all eager to get home now that the first day was over.

"I can give you a ride home at least," Matt said, reaching for her hand.

"That's okay, I want to walk," Elena said, gently disentangling her fingers from his. "I've got some thinking to do. And you've got to get ready for practice, don't you?" She kissed him gently on the cheek, like a sister might instead of a girlfriend, and walked away.

Matt didn't object, but Elena could feel his puzzled gaze following her all the way down the hall toward the school doors.

*Poor Matt*, she thought, sighing. They'd been good friends for so long. Junior year, she'd hoped that he was the boy for her. The one who could be more to her than a trophy or an accessory. And he had been in so many ways—but she hadn't been in love with him, and she hadn't been able to see then how much he loved her.

It had taken Matt a long time to get over her the first time. Maybe that was something else she could fix while she was back here, Elena thought, resisting the urge to turn around and look at him again. If she handled their breakup better ...

She pushed through the front doors of the school and set off. Crossing the parking lot, she tilted her face up toward the warmth of the late afternoon sun and hesitated for a moment.

Her biggest problem right now was how to approach Damon in the right way. If she was going to get him to fall in love with her before Halloween, she had better get started.

Tucking a stray hair back behind her ear, Elena turned down the sidewalk toward home and began to go over her first memories of him, ignoring the chatter of the other students leaving school all around her. He'd come to her in the school gymnasium once, while she and her friends were planning the Haunted House, but that was after she knew Stefan. She didn't know if Damon would have come after her at school if not for Stefan. It wasn't really Damon's kind of place.

She'd met him at Alaric's house at the party Alaric had thrown looking for evidence of vampires. But Alaric wasn't here, wouldn't be here if she accomplished her mission, because he had come after Mr. Tanner was murdered.

She'd sat through history class today, watched as Mr. Tanner mocked Bonnie for her lack of knowledge of history, as Stefan cooly put him in his place. She was struck by how *young* Mr. Tanner was—about the same age as Elena and her friends were in her real present. He was inexperienced and desperate to keep the attention and respect of a class of kids only a few years younger than he was. But despite all that, he'd known a lot about the Renaissance and spoken well about it. Maybe in a few years, he'd be a good teacher. If he lived.

With renewed purpose, Elena walked faster, thinking hard. Damon had come to Bonnie's house. But that was when he was looking for Elena, after she'd already gotten his attention.

A caw came overhead. Elena stopped short and craned her head back to catch a glimpse of a fat black crow in the maple tree overhead. It wasn't Damon, she saw immediately. This bird was plumper, smaller. Probably just a bird, she told herself as it cawed again and then spread its wings and flew off, low, past the house behind her.

But the sight prompted the memory of a dark shape winging its way up from the oak trees at the edge of the cemetery, when she had gone there to visit her parents, before she had known Damon. He'd been keeping an eye on her, hadn't he?

Elena stopped dead. *The cemetery.*

The horrors of her senior year hadn't begun with Mr. Tanner's death on Halloween. They'd begun *today*— when Stefan had fed from an old vagrant sheltering under Wickery Bridge. And it had happened because Stefan had watched Elena in the cemetery, then been caught by a wave of angry Power, leaving him dazed and ravenous.

Katherine's Power, which she had unleashed after witnessing Stefan's interest in Elena, driving Elena out of the churchyard.

The man hadn't died, but his injuries had been the first sign to the people of Fell's Church that danger lurked in their idyllic little town.

Hesitantly, Elena took a few steps toward home. If she didn't go to her parents' graves, the attack wouldn't happen. The old man would be fine, the townwide panic wouldn't begin.

And yet ... Elena stopped again and rocked back on her heels, thinking.

She hadn't been talking to Stefan, hadn't shown any interest in him this time. He wouldn't be following her, would he? And the graveyard would be a good place to try to find Damon. That was the most important thing.

A cloud passed over the sun, and Elena felt a little colder, a little sadder. It had been a long time since she had visited her parents. Now that she lived a few hours away, she hardly ever made it back to Fell's Church. She could see them now, she thought longingly. The cemetery would be isolated and peaceful after her long day. She could be alone there, and Damon would be more likely to come to her when she was alone. Making up her mind, Elena hitched her backpack higher on her shoulders, and headed toward the cemetery, her steps sounding loud and firm in her own ears.

It was a fairly long walk, almost to the edge of town. Coming close to Wickery Bridge, another rusty caw grabbed her attention. Wings spread wide, the huge crow glided to land on the bridge's parapet. Turning its head, it fixed one bright eye on Elena. It seemed to be waiting.

Elena smiled. *Challenge accepted, Damon.*

She had expected to be a little shaky crossing Wickery Bridge, the place where Katherine had pursued her, and Elena had driven off this bridge and drowned. She could still remember the horrible rending sound as the hood of Matt's car had smashed through the old bridge's side. She could almost feel how icy-cold the water had been as she struggled.

But with Damon here, she could be brave.

"Hello, bird," she said casually. The crow stayed very still, its shining dark gaze fixed on Elena. She glanced up at the blue sky, and back at the crow. Then, slowly and deliberately, holding the crow's gaze, Elena smiled, a smile full of secrets. And then she walked on, straight past him, her head high. The bird watched as she passed.

As she entered the cemetery, Elena's gaze fell on the ruined church, and she felt a tremor of foreboding deep inside her. Katherine was down there in the dark passages of the crypts already, watching them all.

At the thought of Katherine, Elena's hands automatically clenched into fists, anxiety running through her. Katherine had been furious when Stefan and Elena had fallen in love, and had attacked them both, had gone after the whole town. It had been the beginning of everything terrible.

Elena's fingernails bit into her palms. How would Katherine feel when Elena went after Damon? Katherine considered both the Salvatores her property, Elena knew, but she had always thought the vampire girl was more possessive of Stefan. She'd even offered to let him live, if he left Damon and Elena to die. But Elena couldn't let herself forget that Katherine was a threat, whichever Salvatore brother Elena pursued.

Crossing past the old church, Elena lifted her chin defiantly. She'd have to solve the Katherine problem when she got to it.

Reaching the newer, well-kept part of the cemetery, Elena rested a hand on the big marble headstone with GILBERT carved into the front.

"Hi, Mom. Hi, Dad," she whispered. "I'm sorry it's been such a long time."

She missed them so much, not as sharply or painfully as when she'd been in high school the first time, but with a powerfully wistful longing. If her beautiful, artistic mother had lived, she could have guided Elena through those first rocky days of being an Earthly Guardian. If her funny, warm father had been there, she could have leaned on him through all the hard times. They would have liked Stefan, she thought, and they would have seen how Damon's stubborn, fiery nature complemented Elena's own.

She wished that she could have gone even further back, that the Guardians had sent her back to Fell's Church when she was twelve. She could have saved her parents. She could have kept them out of the car that terrible day that had ended their lives and changed hers and Margaret's forever.

With a powerful rush of longing, Elena remembered her mother laughing as she chased her through the house when Elena had been very small, catching her and sweeping her up into her arms for a hug.

"I still miss you," she whispered, brushing her hand across her parents' names.

A sudden wind caught her hair, whipping it across her face. Looking up, Elena saw the tops of the oak trees at the edge of the cemetery tossing violently. Dark clouds were massing above her, and there was a sharp chill in the air. She shivered.

The sky grew darker still. This wasn't a natural storm, surely. It had been clear and sunny only a moment before.

Damon? He could change the weather when he wanted to. Or Katherine? She was far more powerful than Damon right now.

Elena shuddered. If it was Katherine, she might kill Elena without even thinking about it. She remembered how easily Katherine had torn Damon's chest apart with her long talonlike nails, as her fangs ripped through his throat. There had been so much blood.

Elena steeled herself. Running wouldn't make any difference; she knew that this time. She'd tried that, and Katherine had caught up with her eventually. Again, she remembered the cold of the water under Wickery Bridge and shivered.

"I'm not afraid," she said stubbornly. "Whatever's out there, I'm ready for you."

The wind stopped. Everything grew still, the leaves hanging motionless from the trees. All around Elena was silence, without even the chirp of a bird or the sound of a car in the distance.

Something stirred in the shadows under the oak trees. Elena squinted, trying to see. A dark figure moved toward her. The dim sunlight caught pale skin and sleek, night-dark hair. Black boots, black jeans, black shirt, black leather jacket. An arrogant lift to his chin, as if he'd seen everything in the world and didn't think much of it. Damon.

Thunder crashed overhead and Elena, despite herself, jumped.

"Nervous?" Damon was smiling faintly, his dark eyes amused. He was so beautiful, she thought absently. That was always true, always had been true. Sculpted cheekbones and clean, fine features. But there was something unfamiliar in that smile. There was none of the affection, none of the tenderness she was used to.

Elena reached for the bond between them automatically, wanting to check on Damon's thoughts and emotions, and to reaffirm their constant connection. But there was nothing. The Guardian's bond didn't exist here.

Damon moved closer, his eyes fixed on her face. "There's a storm coming," he said, his voice low and intimate, as if he was telling her a secret. The thunder grumbled again. "A bad day for a walk."

Elena felt her own smile rise to meet his challenging one. "I'm not afraid of a little rain," she said.

"No, I imagine you're not afraid of much." Damon lifted a hand to brush Elena's cheek, tracing a finger lightly down her throat. He was far too close, and something twisted uneasily inside Elena.

This was Damon. She had no reason to fear him. Damon *loved* her.

Only … not this Damon. Not yet. This Damon was a hunter, and he was looking at Elena as if she were prey. Despite herself, she stepped backward.

His eyes narrowed and his smile spread. Elena jutted her chin out stubbornly. She was not going to flinch away from Damon. She wouldn't give him the satisfaction.

"Someone could be watching you," Damon went on, moving closer still. "A young girl, alone in a graveyard, when night is beginning to fall." His voice was soothing, hypnotic almost, and he moved toward her once more, so close that she could feel his breath on her skin.

Elena's chest ached. This wasn't her Damon, this Damon with the cruel set to his mouth and the malicious gleam in his eyes. He was dangerous, even to her.

But, after all, he *was* Damon, wasn't he? He didn't know her, not yet, but Elena knew *him*, inside and out. She felt a smile blossoming on her own face and her shoulders, which had lifted as if she was expecting a blow, dropped.

"It's all right," she said. "I know you'd never hurt me."

Damon frowned and took a step back away from her. He hesitated for a split second, then opened his mouth to speak.

"Elena?" Startled, Elena turned to see Bonnie and Meredith approaching from the other end of the graveyard. "Elena?" Bonnie called again.

A light breeze broke the stillness of the air, lifting Elena's hair. The sun came out from behind the dark clouds, and a mockingbird sang an insistent trill from a nearby tree. A cool finger brushed across the nape of Elena's neck. She gasped and whipped back around, but Damon was gone. The green grass over the graves behind her was as smooth and empty as if he had never been there.

"Elena," Bonnie said as they reached Elena, "sometimes I *worry* about you. I really do."

"Was somebody here?" Meredith said, confusion on her face. "I thought ..." Had Damon Influenced them to forget him? Elena wondered. Or had he simply moved so quickly they weren't sure what they had seen?

"It's just me," Elena said slowly, her eyes still searching the graveyard. There were no dark figures among the trees. No black bird rose toward the sky. "I didn't expect you guys to follow me."

"You can tell us to go away," Meredith suggested, glancing at the gray stone above Elena's parents' graves.

Elena shook her head. "It's okay," she said. "I wanted to hang out with you guys anyway." She sat down in the sun-warmed grass beside the headstone, pulling the others down next to her. The three girls sat quietly for a while, watching the soft white clouds blow across the sky.

Bonnie ran her fingers through Elena's ponytail, taking the ribbon out and twining it into little braids. The gentle pulls on her hair felt good, and Elena relaxed, leaning back against her friend's leg.

"So," Bonnie started, her hands not pausing in their braiding, "are you going to tell us why you've been acting so funny today?"

Elena opened her mouth, a denial springing to her lips, and caught Meredith's knowing gaze.

"I know I said you seemed distracted this morning," Meredith told her, "but it's more than that."

"You've been getting the strangest look on your face when you look at people, even us," Bonnie said thoughtfully, tucking a stray piece of hair into one of Elena's braids. "Like *we're* strangers."

Elena turned at that, her hair slipping through Bonnie's fingers, and looked at her friend. Bonnie stared back at her, brown eyes wide and a little hurt.

"It's not like that." Elena said. But it did feel, a little bit, like they were different people from the ones she knew. Bonnie and Meredith had been through so much with her—they'd even traveled to a different dimension together—but not yet, not *this* Bonnie and Meredith.

If Elena managed to change what happened now, if she could keep Damon from killing Mr. Tanner and setting the future she already knew in motion, would her friendship with Bonnie and Meredith change, too? She ached with sorrow at the idea.

"If something's wrong, we want to help," Meredith said softly.

Warmth ran through Elena, soothing away that sorrowful ache, and she reached for her friends' hands. "I'm fine," she said, gripping Bonnie's square, small hand and Meredith's long cool one. "Only … everything's changing, isn't it? It's our senior year, our last year together."

"Nothing's going to change," Bonnie said uncomfortably. "Nothing important. Just school and stuff."

"Elena's right," Meredith said, turning her hand to thread her fingers through Elena's. "Next year at this time, who knows where we'll all be?"

"You've both been such good friends to me," Elena said in a rush. "When my parents died … I couldn't have gotten through that bad time without you. I don't want to lose you guys, not ever."

Bonnie sniffed and pulled away from Elena to wipe at her eyes. "Don't make me cry," she said, half laughing. "My mascara will run, and then I'll look like a raccoon."

"Let's swear an oath." Elena said determinedly. "An oath that we'll always be true friends."

They'd sworn a blood oath in this graveyard the first time she'd lived this. Bonnie and Meredith had sworn that they would do anything Elena asked in relation to Stefan. And Elena had sworn not to rest until Stefan belonged to her. Not even if it killed her.

And, well, it had killed her in the end, hadn't it? It had killed both of them. An oath like that—sworn in blood in a graveyard—had true Power.

"Wait a minute," Meredith said, as Elena had known she would. She let go of Elena's hand and unfastened a pin from her blouse, then jabbed it quickly into her thumb. "Bonnie, give me your hand."

"Why?" Bonnie asked, frowning suspiciously at the pin.

"Because I want to marry you," Meredith said sarcastically, and Elena smiled a little. "Why do you think?"

"But—but—Oh, all *right*. Ow!"

"Now you, Elena." Meredith hesitated and then jabbed at Elena's finger, their eyes meeting for a moment. She held out her own thumb, a plump drop of blood swelling on its pad, and Bonnie and Elena pressed their thumbs against hers. Bonnie's eyes were still shining with tears and Meredith looked pale and earnest. Affection for them both swelled inside Elena. These were her *sisters*.

"I swear that I'll always be there for both of you," Meredith said steadily. "I'll be on your side and do every-thing I can for you, no matter what happens."

"No matter what," Bonnie said, closing her eyes. "I swear."

Elena, pressing her thumb hard against the other girls', ignoring the twinge of pain, said softly, "I swear, I will always be there for you, no matter what." She felt breathless and expectant. This was sacred.

A gust of cold wind blew through the cemetery, lifting the girls' hair, and sending a flurry of dry leaves across the ground. Bonnie gasped and pulled back, and they all giggled. A flush of satisfaction filled Elena. Whatever happened, however the world changed now, at least she knew she'd have Bonnie and Meredith.

## 8

Elena rested her head in her hands, staring down at the scratched surface of her desk as her classmates settled into their seats for trigonometry class. Ignoring their chatter, she went back over her meeting with Damon in the graveyard the day before. Was there something she should have done differently?

She knew she'd intrigued him. She had seen his pupils widen when he leaned in toward her, his eyes curious and hungry. She'd half expected him to appear at her window that night. But he hadn't.

Although ... that morning she'd heard the caw of a crow and whipped around just too late to see the bird. All the way to school, she'd had the disquieting feeling that she was being watched.

Halloween was coming. The night Damon had killed Mr. Tanner. Shifting uneasily in her seat, Elena remembered how Mr. Tanner's head had flopped lifelessly backward against the altar in the Halloween house of horrors. His throat had been caked with blood. Elena squeezed her eyes shut tight, trying to block out the memories.

Damon had been at the Haunted House that night, and seeing Elena and Stefan together filled him with jealousy and seething resentment. He had lashed out by feeding on Mr. Tanner when Mr. Tanner stuck a dagger into him. Damon had killed him out of surprised rage and pain.

According to Mylea, that was when Damon's fate had been sealed. If Elena didn't manage to change what happened, she would die. Stefan would die. And Elena couldn't imagine the Guardians would let Damon live, not without Elena to rein him in. They would all be doomed.

So far, she'd successfully avoided Stefan. In history class she tried to close her mind off, scowling with concentration as she chanted multiplication tables or dialogue from old movies in her mind—anything to drown out whatever part of her might call to Stefan. He didn't try to talk to her, either. She'd had to pursue him last time; he hadn't wanted to be reminded of Katherine, hadn't wanted to connect with her.

But Elena could feel him watching her in the halls, as clearly as she could feel Damon watching her on the streets. The other day, she'd glanced at Stefan in class without meaning to and seen his green eyes fixed on her. His gaze had been soft and longing, *hungry*. She wanted to comfort him, but Elena already knew how that would end.

The speaker set high on the classroom wall crackled, jolting Elena out of her thoughts. She half listened to the morning announcements, snapping to attention as the vice principal's voice said, "Senior Homecoming Court nominations have been tallied. This year's nominees for Homecoming Queen are Sue Carson, Caroline Forbes, Elena Gilbert, Bonnie McCullough, and Meredith Sulez. Voting will take place in the cafeteria over the next week. Congratulations to all the nominees."

Elena gripped the edge of her desk, a sudden panic running through her. No. No way.

*Homecoming* had been when it all began. A dizzying whirl of images rose up in Elena's mind's eye. Herself, determined that Stefan wouldn't turn her down. Leaving the dance in Tyler Smallwood's convertible, the taste of whiskey sharp in her mouth, her hair blowing wildly in the wind as they sped down the highway. The lid of the tomb in the ruined church shifting under her hand. The ripping sound as Tyler tore her dress.

Stefan saving her, taking her in his arms. Her whole world changing.

She couldn't let it happen again.

"Congratulations, girls," Mrs. Halpern said to Meredith and Elena as the speaker clicked off. "There's a meeting for all the Homecoming Court nominees with the faculty sponsors in the office third period."

Elena raised her hand. "Mrs. Halpern," she said. "I don't want to be on the Homecoming Court. Is there something I have to do to drop out of the race?" She heard Meredith's gasp of surprise behind her.

There was a moment of utter silence as everyone contemplated the thought. Elena Gilbert, queen of the school, refusing to compete? She was sure to win, they all knew that.

"Uh, no," Mrs. Halpern said, her forehead crinkled in a puzzled frown. "If you're sure, Elena, I can just let the sponsors know." At Elena's nod, she made a note on her clipboard.

Ignoring the whispers around her, Elena waited out the rest of the period. When the bell rang, she pretended not to see Meredith striding toward her and slipped out the door alone. She would have to figure out some kind of explanation to give Bonnie and Meredith.

Outside, Matt was waiting, a smile stretching across his handsome, all-American face. "Congratulations," he said, pulling her close and kissing her easily, just a sweet press of his lips. "You're a shoo-in for Queen. Tell me what color dress you're wearing, and I'll make sure to get the right kind of corsage." Despite his words, there was a wary look in his eyes, as if he was bracing himself for a blow.

"Oh, Matt," Elena said, feeling stricken. She'd been avoiding him, avoiding this moment, and of course he'd noticed.

Whatever happened, her relationship with Matt was over, and she couldn't keep him hanging on. She needed to let him go, kindly, before she went after Damon.

The smile slipped off Matt's face, and he bowed his head. "I'm guessing you've got something to tell me, huh?"

Elena pulled him aside into a little alcove past the lockers, ignoring the curious looks of students passing by. It wasn't nice—it wasn't fair—to spring this on him here, right in the middle of the school day, but she couldn't string Matt along any longer.

"I *do* love you," she said in a fierce whisper, when they were as private as they could be. "I do."

Matt flinched a little and then gave Elena a smile that was almost a grimace. "I guess that's why you're dumping me, huh? Because I'm just that loveable. I should have realized before." His voice was hoarse and, spontaneously, Elena wrapped her arms around him, pushing her face against the rough fabric of his letterman's jacket.

Unbidden tears rose in her eyes. "Oh, Matt," she said, muffled against his shoulder. "You're my friend. My true friend. Don't love me like this anymore."

Matt sighed and stroked the back of Elena's head, running his strong fingers through her hair. "It's not that easy, Elena. I can't just stop how I feel. But I won't try to hold onto you, not if you don't want me to."

When she lifted her head to look at him, there was devastation on his face, beneath the steady eyes and the crooked grin. How had she not seen this the first time? She barely remembered this conversation. It had just been a means to an end: getting Matt squared away so that she had an open field to go after Stefan.

A curl of self-disgust twisted inside Elena, and she lowered her head again, wiping her eyes against Matt's shoulder. She'd gone through this part of her life with blinders on. And poor Matt, once he'd gotten over her, his next girlfriend had become a vampire and finally killed herself. All the craziness here—Fell's Church, Dalcrest, all along the ley lines—had ruined so much of Matt's life.

When she pulled back from their hug, Matt was staring at her, his forehead creased with concern. "Are you all right?" he asked.

Elena bit her lip to keep back a hysterical giggle. If she kept up with these mood swings, remembering the future that might not come, everyone was going to think she was having a nervous breakdown. "Listen, Matt," she said, "we're good friends, we really are. I love you so much. But there's nothing for you here. As soon as we're out of school, you should go. Take a football scholarship. You're bound to get one."

He had been offered one, hadn't he? A good one, at some big football school. And he'd turned it down. He'd come to Dalcrest to help them protect the innocent.

Elena thought of Jasmine, with her easy smile and soft eyes, her fiercely loyal heart. "You'll meet the right person for you someday," she told him, trying to make him believe. "She'll be smart and kind, and it'll be so much better than we could have been together."

The smile was gone from Matt's face. "You're the only person I want to be with," he said flatly. His eyes narrowed. "Does this have anything to do with the new guy? He's always watching you."

"Stefan?" Matt had always seen more than she'd given him credit for. Elena met his gaze squarely. "I don't want to date Stefan Salvatore," she said honestly, and after a moment, Matt nodded, his shoulders slumping.

"I guess there doesn't have to be someone else for you to break up with me," he said. "You always know what you want, Elena. And what you don't."

"You're one of my best friends," Elena told him. "I just want the best for you."

Matt shook his head, confused. "You're different since you came back from France," he said. Then the corners of his mouth tilted up in a small, sad smile. "Maybe the trip was good for you, too."

\* \* \*

"But if you broke up with Matt, who are you going to go to Homecoming with?" Bonnie asked after school, as they turned down the walk to Bonnie's house. It was a warm afternoon, and Bonnie had invited Meredith and Elena over to hang out.

"I don't know," Elena said. "Does it matter?"

Meredith and Bonnie stared at her with identical expressions of shock.

"Does it—" Bonnie echoed incredulously.

"Elena, is there something *wrong* with you?" Meredith interrupted. "You're really not acting like yourself."

Feeling defensive, Elena shrugged. "I guess I just don't think Homecoming is all that important."

"That's what she means when she says you're not acting like yourself," Bonnie said tartly, opening the front door.

Yangtze, Bonnie's family's fat, elderly Pekingese, greeted them with shrill, yapping barks, trying to wiggle his chubby body out through the open door. Bonnie pushed him back, and he growled and snapped at Elena's ankle as she went by.

Katherine had killed Yangtze, Elena remembered. Bonnie's mother had cried off and on for days. The dog was so spoiled, she was the only one who could stand him. But there had been no sign of Katherine in the cemetery the other evening, no wild surge of Power to send the girls running screaming across Wickery Bridge. Maybe if Elena and Stefan didn't fall in love, none of the terrible things from Elena's first time around—not even Yangtze's death—would happen.

Gingerly, Elena reached down and patted the dog's back, earning another snarl. But wait, she thought, pulling back her hand. If Yangtze didn't die, wouldn't the world be different, in ways Elena couldn't even predict? The dog was the smallest part of all this, but every piece of the world made a difference.

Something terrible might happen, Elena thought, suddenly cold with panic. What if Bonnie tripped over the dog's small, round body on the stairs and fell, cracked her spine, and wound up in a wheelchair? What if the dog finally managed to push its way out, ran into the road, and caused a fatal car accident? *Anything could happen.* At the realization, all the breath went out of Elena's body in a sudden gasp, and she clapped her hand over her mouth.

"What is it?" Meredith asked warily, but Elena just shook her head, her mind spinning. Anything could happen. The

Guardian had told her that, but she hadn't really thought about it. Elena was changing everyone's lives, and what if she accidentally changed them for the worse? At least in Elena's own reality, Bonnie, Meredith, and Matt were more or less safe.

Not Stefan, though. Stefan had died.

Not Elena, who was dying.

And not Damon. She was the last one he had left. For a long time, Stefan had been the only person in the world Damon gave a damn about. And then Elena had come, and their bond had tethered Damon to her, to humanity. And now, in her reality, Elena was dying and Damon was losing the last bit of that humanity he had left.

In the McCullough's living room, Bonnie's sister Mary was unpinning a nurse's cap from her wavy red hair. "Hey girls," she said, dropping her cap on the table. She looked exhausted, dark circles under her eyes.

"Long shift?" Bonnie asked. Mary worked at the Fell's Church clinic, which was always busy.

Mary sighed and closed her eyes for a second. "We got a pretty bad case in today," she said. "You girls go down to the cemetery sometimes, don't you? Down by the Wickery Bridge?"

"Well, sure," Bonnie said slowly. This wasn't something they talked about. "Elena's parents ..."

"That's what I thought." Mary took a deep breath. "Listen to me, Bonnie. Don't ever, *ever* go out there again. Especially not alone or at night."

"Why?" Bonnie asked, bewildered.

Elena's stomach clenched. It shouldn't have happened. Things had been different this time, down near Wickery Bridge.

"Last night somebody was attacked out there," Mary said. "They found him right under Wickery Bridge."

Meredith and Bonnie stared at her in disbelief, and Elena with a dull, wondering dread. Bonnie clutched Elena's arm, her fingers pinching painfully tight. "Somebody was attacked under the bridge? Who? What happened?"

"I don't know," Mary said, shaking her head. "This morning one of the cemetery workers spotted him lying there. He was some homeless person, I guess. He was probably sleeping under the bridge when he was attacked. But he was half-dead when they found him, and he's still unconscious. He might die."

*Stefan.* Elena felt weighed down by guilt. She had thought things had changed. Was Stefan following Elena in this reality, too? Had he been overcome with the need for blood and attacked the homeless man anyway?

Or was it Damon who had attacked the man under the bridge? Damon had been at the cemetery.

Maybe fate wasn't changeable after all, Elena thought, chilled. Maybe the man had been destined to be terribly hurt that night at the bridge, no matter what.

If so, perhaps her mission was doomed to failure. Maybe she and Stefan and Damon would continue on the same path, no matter how she tried to alter things. It was possible, wasn't it, that all roads would end with Stefan falling, a false friend's stave in his heart, with Elena drifting to death in her big white bed? With Damon's heart breaking, all his steps toward redemption lost?

"His throat was nearly ripped out," Mary said grimly. "He lost an incredible amount of blood. They thought it might have been an animal at first, but now Dr. Lowen says it was a person. And the police think whoever did it may be hiding in the cemetery." She looked at each of them, her mouth tight.

"You don't have to scare us," Bonnie said, her voice strained. "We get the point, Mary."

"All right. Good." Mary rubbed the back of her neck and sighed. "I've got to lie down for a while. I didn't mean to be crabby." She left the living room, heading for the stairs.

"It could have been one of us." Meredith said. She bit her lip. "Especially you, Elena. You went there alone."

"No," Elena said absently. "It would never have been one of us." She barely noticed the way the other girls stared at her, shocked by the certainty in her voice.

Elena clenched her fists, her nails biting into the palms of her hands. It couldn't all be inevitable. There was a way to save Mr. Tanner, a way to keep the town safe from all the havoc Katherine, Damon, and Stefan had, in their own separate ways, brought down upon it.

She had to find Damon, and soon. Halloween was coming fast, and she would need time with him if he was going to fall in love with her, if she was going to show him there were things more pleasurable than destruction.

Elena needed a plan.

## 9

A chilly breeze swept through Elena's hair, and she wrapped her arms around herself for warmth. The sun hadn't set yet, but there was already a pale moon high in the sky, and dark shadows were spreading under the trees.

She'd really thought Damon would have come to her by now. Elena had made excuses to dodge Bonnie and Meredith after school, and headed out to the woods. She had to draw Damon to her again, needed to start building a connection between them. And here, isolated beneath the ancient oak trees, was just where he was likely to appear.

A bird crashed through the top of the tree above her, and Elena looked up with a burst of relief. But it was just a blue jay, not the sleek black crow she was waiting for.

Maybe she should give up on subtlety and just shout Damon's name until he answered her. No, that would only make him suspicious.

If he was nearby, there was one thing that ought to draw him out. Blood.

Elena uncrossed her arms and looked around carefully. A rough gray boulder lay half-buried between two trees with twisted roots growing up around it. That might do. Steeling herself, Elena wandered toward it.

Her toe caught on a root, and Elena tipped forward, eyeing the sharp-edged rock. *About right.* Pretending to lose her balance, she threw herself onto the ground hard.

Her teeth clacked together as she hit the ground more violently than she'd meant to. There was a jolting, blinding pain in her knee. Her palms were stinging, scraped by tree roots. Winded, Elena lay gasping for a moment, fighting back tears of pain. She glanced down at her leg and was relieved to see a trickle of red blood. She didn't want to have to try that again.

"Let me help you." The voice, husky and a little unsure, was so familiar, so loved. But it was the wrong one.

Elena looked up to see Stefan Salvatore standing above her, his hand extended. His face was shadowed so that she couldn't quite see his expression. Tentatively, she laid her hand in his and let him pull her gently to her feet.

Upright again, she winced a little, and Stefan quickly turned her hands palm-up, carefully brushing away dirt and bits of dry leaves. "Just a scrape," he told her quietly.

"My leg," she said, looking up into his face. Her voice cracked, and she had to swallow hard. He hadn't changed. Of course he never changed; he was a vampire. Elena's heart ached, and for one mad moment, she wanted to forget everything and throw herself into his arms and hold him tightly, weep with joy that he was alive.

"Let me see," Stefan said, letting go of her hands. He didn't look her in the eyes, but instead knelt in the dirt, pulling a white silk handkerchief from his pocket. Unfolding it, he tucked something small—Elena couldn't see what it was—back into his pocket. Gently, he blotted at her knee and then tied the handkerchief around it as a makeshift bandage. "There, that should get you home."

He rose, eyes still averted, and backed away. Impulsively, Elena stepped forward and took hold of his leather-jacketed arm. He was so close, so solid, and *real*. A warm flush of love and relief ran over her. "Thank you," she said. "Stefan—"

Almost faster than her eyes could follow, Stefan pulled away from her, and stepped back, deeper into the shadows of the trees. "I—" he said and stopped, then began again. "You're welcome. You should be careful, though, out here alone. Did you hear about the attack?"

"Yes, I did," Elena said, moving closer to him again, her eyes searching the shadows, trying to make out his face.

"They're saying whoever did it must have been a monster." There was an ugly, harsh note in Stefan's voice. Without the sunglasses, he looked vulnerable and terribly tired.

"I don't believe it," she said firmly.

For a moment, their eyes met. Elena could see a wild flicker of hope rise in Stefan's and then disappear, leaving nothing but grim hopelessness. "Anyone who would do such a thing is a monster," he said.

Elena was almost touching him now. She wanted to run her hands across the chiseled lines of his face, remind herself how smooth his skin was.

His gaze traced over the curve of her neck, she saw, and his lips parted a little. "You look—" he said. "You remind me of someone I used to know."

*Katherine.* Elena suppressed a grimace. The Stefan of this time was still guilt-stricken over the role he thought he'd played in Katherine's death. She wanted to announce the truth: *She's not dead. Crazy and vicious, but not dead. It's not your fault.*

But she couldn't. There was no way she could know that now, or at least no way she could explain. And so, Elena said nothing. Instead, she reached out a hand, slowly, carefully, as if she was taming some wild creature, and finally touched him. Just for a moment, her fingers brushing across the bare skin of his wrist.

She couldn't have him. But this—a moment of touch—she needed.

It was like a circuit connecting. Warmth flooded through Elena's body, and she wobbled for a moment, ready to fall into his arms. Stefan became utterly still, his eyes dilated and dark as he stared at her. She thought he was holding his breath. There was a moment when it seemed like time was suspended, like anything could happen.

And then, with an intense jolt of sorrow, Elena pulled away, letting her hand fall limply to her side.

"Here," Stefan said abruptly, pulling something from his pocket with the sleeve of his shirt. His voice shook, and he was staring at his hands, refusing to meet Elena's eye. He handed her what looked like a handful of scrappy, skinny weeds, a few with small pale flowers. "Keep these with you for good luck. You can even make herbal tea out of them."

Elena accepted the flowers, recognizing them as vervain. If she kept it close, it would keep vampires from being able to cloud her mind. But Stefan didn't know yet that Damon was in town, certainly didn't know about Katherine. Who was he protecting her from? Then she got it.

Himself, of course. It was just like Stefan, to be thinking of himself as a danger while he did everything he could to protect her.

"Thank you," she said, looking down at the wilting weeds as if they were the most precious thing she'd ever touched.

She stared up at him again, holding her gaze until, reluctantly, he let his eyes meet hers again. "Remember," she said softly. "I don't believe in monsters."

Stefan's face twisted, and he turned and walked away, disappearing into the gathering dusk.

Elena sighed and tucked the vervain into her pocket before heading home. She felt safe, despite the dark. Even if she couldn't see him, Stefan would guard her carefully all the way home.

#TVD13StelenaReturns

*inety-seven. Ninety-eight.* Elena brushed her hair with smooth, even strokes, watching herself in the elaborately framed Victorian mirror above her dresser. She met her own reflected gaze levely, her dark blue eyes as steady as her hand on the hairbrush. Her golden hair fanned out like silk across her shoulders.

It was odd, she thought, that she looked almost exactly the same here as she did in her own time. Her friends were younger, softer, but Elena's appearance hadn't changed since she had drunk the Water of Eternal Life and Youth back in her freshman year of college. When she had chosen to be with Stefan forever.

She was *not* going to think about Stefan.

Her hand slowed and her eyes dropped.

There was still that instant fire between them. The rest of the world melted away when she was with Stefan. It had felt so right, so perfect, to talk to him and touch him again.

But it didn't matter. She had to stay away from Stefan. It didn't matter how much she yearned to be with him. She couldn't get caught in that trap. Giving in to her love for Stefan led, in the end, to death and despair. There was a reason she was here.

She put the brush down on top of her rosewood dresser, lining it up neatly between her jewelry box and her comb, and reached into the top shelf of the dresser for a lacy white nightgown. The house was silent. Aunt Judith and Margaret were already fast asleep, but Elena was buzzing with nervous energy. Still, she should try to rest.

Suddenly, there was a rap at the window, a sharp, cracking noise. Elena spun around. Outside, she could just make out a pale face in the darkness, hair and clothes as black as the night around him. *Damon.*

"Let me in." The low, coaxing voice sent a shiver up Elena's spine. She didn't move. "Open the window, Elena. You want to let me inside."

He was trying to *compel* her? A hot flush of anger ran over her. In two quick steps, she crossed the room and flung the window open.

Damon's eyes widened a bit. She knew she wasn't moving in the dreamy way a compelled person usually would, but the corners of his lush mouth tilted, and Elena could tell he'd decided to go with it. "Good," he said, his tone soothing, "Now, invite me in, Princess."

Elena folded her arms in front of her. "I don't know if I should," she said slowly. Her heart was pounding. Gratefully, she thought of the withered vervain in her pocket.

Cocking his head to one side, Damon eyed her thoughtfully. Sitting on a branch of the quince tree outside her window, one arm braced on the windowsill, he somehow managed to look as comfortable and graceful as ever. "You've got vervain," he said.

"I do." Elena didn't offer anything else. If she wanted him intrigued by her, it was probably best to leave a little mystery.

Damon's smile sharpened. "Didn't you say you knew I would never hurt you?"

Elena's mouth went dry, and then she swallowed hard and stepped back from the window. This was *Damon*. She was safe. "Come in, then, Damon," she said.

Damon hesitated for just a moment, uncertainty flickering over his face, and then he was through the window smoothly and standing in front of her. "You know my name," he said warily.

"Yes." She didn't try to explain. What could she say? All the things that might make Damon trust her were still in the future.

Damon moved closer. There was something hot and hungry in his gaze, and she had a sudden urge to raise her hand to cover where her pulse beat.

Elena was glad that she was still dressed in the clothes she'd worn to the woods, not the low-necked nightgown in her hand. It would have felt wrong, would have felt *dangerous*, if he had seen her like that right now, her throat so exposed.

"If you're not afraid, come here," he said coaxingly. "Let me taste you." His irises were so dark that she could hardly make out his pupils.

For *her* Damon, the Damon she loved in her own time, Elena would have swept back her hair and bared her throat in an instant, eager for the sweet connection that came with the exchange of blood. Even now, she ached for that feeling.

But no, not yet. *This* Damon wasn't ready to share with her as an equal: He just wanted to take.

Instead, she set her jaw firmly and stared back at him. "You *won't* hurt me," she said. "But I'm not ready for that."

Again, Damon hesitated for a moment, his brow wrinkling. "You know my name *and* you have vervain," he said. He took a step closer to her. "Someone's been telling tales about me."

He was very close to her now, near enough that Elena had to tilt her head back to look up at him, exposing the long lines of her throat. The fine hairs rose on the back of her neck, some small, primitive part of her brain recognizing: *predator*. His gaze was unfriendly. But Elena held her ground.

"No one's told me a thing about you," she said honestly. "I'm just a girl who happens to know a thing or two about vampires. And how to protect myself."

"And my name?" Slowly, Damon raised his hand and ran a finger lightly along Elena's jaw. His touch was gentle, but his gaze was cold, and Elena suppressed a shudder.

"I don't mean you any harm, Damon," she said, looking straight into his eyes. "I might know things, but I would never try to hurt you." She could hear the sincerity in her own voice, and she thought Damon could too, because his hand dropped and he cocked his head, looking at her more closely.

"You look like someone I used to know," he said. "But you're not at all like her."

Elena didn't know what to say to that, so she said nothing. Damon smiled.

"So, you're a girl who knows things," he said, a faint mocking tone in his voice. "A girl who hangs out in grave-yards at dusk and willingly invites vampires into her boudoir. Are you flirting with the darkness, Princess? Do you want to come with me into the night?"

He reached out for Elena and pulled her against him. His eyes were on her throat again, and his fingers dug into her upper arms.

"That's not what I want at all," Elena said, trying to pull away. Her voice sounded startlingly loud to her own ears, and she realized they had been speaking in hushed voices, almost whispering. Damon's gaze flew from her throat to meet her eyes.

"You're wrong," she said, desperately. His fingers were holding her too tightly. "I don't want the darkness. I want you to come into the light with me."

Damon laughed, a sudden burst of laughter, and let her go. The laugh warmed his face, made him look more like *her* Damon, and less like the predator who'd been standing too close to her a moment before.

"What, are you a missionary come to save my soul?" he asked, smiling in what looked like honest delight.

"Maybe." Elena could feel her cheeks turning pink, but she held her head high. "Things are better in the light. I could show you."

Damon laughed again, a low, silky chuckle this time, and, before Elena realized what he was doing, he leaned toward her and brushed his cool, dry lips against hers, just for a second. "You'll see me again, Princess," he whispered, and then, faster than her eyes could follow, he was gone.

Alone in her bedroom, Elena touched her fingers against her lips, her heart pounding wildly.

He wasn't her Damon, not at all. Not yet. He didn't know her, didn't care for her, and that made him danger-ous. For her own safety, she would have to remember that.

## 11

"Will you take me to the park tomorrow?" Margaret asked. She gazed at Elena across the kitchen table with wide blue eyes, her unbrushed dandelion-fluff hair sticking up in all directions. Behind her, Aunt Judith poured cereal into bowls.

"Sure, Meggie," Elena said absently, picking at her toast. Margaret squealed and bounced in her seat. Elena smiled at her sister. They'd go Saturday morning, she decided, just the two of them, before she went dress shopping with Meredith and Bonnie.

Mornings like these were an unexpected blessing of her excursion into the past, Elena thought as she watched Margaret blow bubbles in her milk. She hadn't known to treasure these mundane, everyday moments the first time alive, because she hadn't known how quickly they would end. After this year, she'd never live at home with Margaret and Aunt Judith again. In one possible future—the first one, the one she couldn't help thinking of as the *real* one— Elena would be dead before Christmas.

Aunt Judith set down a glass of orange juice in front of Margaret. "Stop blowing bubbles," she told her firmly. "And, Elena, much as I like having you here for breakfast, you're going to be late for school if you don't get going."

"Oh," Elena said, looking up at the clock. She stood and reached for her backpack reluctantly. There was a quiver of nervousness deep in her stomach at the idea of seeing Stefan again. Until yesterday she'd almost forgotten the exact shade of Stefan's green eyes. Now she thought she might have been better off forgetting when she couldn't look into those eyes every day.

And then there was Damon. She could connect with him, she was sure of it. Damon would change for her. He *had* changed for her. Without Stefan between them, it would happen faster. She just didn't know if it could happen in time. Halloween was coming soon, and she'd only managed two brief and enigmatic conversations with Damon.

"I don't know if I'll be back for dinner," she said, dropping a kiss on Margaret's head. "I might go to Bonnie's house after school. Don't wait for me." Maybe if she went to the cemetery again this evening, Damon would come to her there.

Aunt Judith sighed and handed her an apple. "You hardly had any breakfast. Eat something healthy at lunch."

Elena only nodded. She was thinking of Damon's sharp, brilliant smile, and how quickly it faded. How rough his voice had been when he asked if she wanted to come into the darkness.

She opened the front door, and there, a dark figure against the bright colors of the day, was Damon, as if her thoughts had summoned him. Elena jerked back, her mouth dropping open.

The corners of Damon's mouth tilted up at her surprise. "Hello, Princess," he said lazily, his voice slow and easy. In one hand, he casually held a bouquet of white roses. "Here I am in the light, just like you wanted." He held the roses out to her, his smile mocking.

"Thank you, they're beautiful," Elena said hesitantly.

She stepped back and headed for the kitchen. "You can come in," she said over her shoulder. This was technically a different house than she'd invited him into last night. Her bedroom and the living room were the only remains of the original house, the one that had almost completely burned in the Civil War.

Perhaps, she thought, hearing his soft footsteps behind her, she should have kept him out. But he had never hurt

Margaret or Aunt Judith. She had to show that she trusted Damon if she expected him to start trusting her.

In the kitchen, Elena reached into a high cupboard to take out a vase and began to fill it with water.

"Elena?" Aunt Judith asked. "You'll be late—" She stopped in surprise as Damon came through the doorway.

"Look what Damon brought me," Elena said lightly. Damon turned on his most brilliant smile and held out his hand.

"Damon Salvatore," he said, introducing himself. "I'll drive Elena to school today, make sure she gets there on time."

Flustered, Aunt Judith reached up to smooth her hair before taking Damon's hand. "Pleased to meet you," she said, shooting Elena a look that said, as clearly as words, *Who is this? What happened to Matt?*

Elena plopped the flowers into the vase and took a few minutes to arrange them neatly, half listening to Damon and Aunt Judith's conversation behind her.

"At university," Damon was telling Aunt Judith. "I'm just here to visit family. Fell's Church is lovely." His voice was, if anything, a little too polite. And there was a familiar note in it, almost coaxing. Elena's fingers stiffened on the rose stems. Was Damon using his Power on Aunt Judith? Aunt Judith and her fiancé, Robert, had always liked Damon. Was that because Damon had cheated? She hadn't realized he would use his Power so casually. She swung around to stare at him. Damon met her eyes innocently, a bland smile on his lips.

Behind him, Margaret stared at Damon from the kitchen table. "Aunt Judith?" the little girl asked, her voice quavering. Perhaps she could sense Damon's will working on Aunt Judith, compelling her to welcome him here.

"Let's go," Elena told Damon sharply.

"Certainly," he said, still smiling. "You don't want to be late to class." He nodded politely to Aunt Judith.

Elena set the vase of roses down on the table, a little harder than she needed to, and kissed her aunt on the cheek. "See you later."

Damon followed Elena to the front door. "Now that you've got the roses, perhaps you should leave those little flowering weeds in your pocket behind," he said idly.

"Very funny," Elena said, opening the door and turning to look at him. She was aware of the vervain nestled deep in her pocket, but it was interesting that Damon could sense it as well. Or perhaps he was only guessing. "The roses are gorgeous, though," she added, and Damon's lips curved into a smile.

The car parked outside was *amazing*: low, sleek, and clearly very expensive. Damon opened the door for her.

"Are you sure you want to go to school today, Princess?" he asked. "There's a whole wide world out there. You could show me around Fell's Church."

"It's tempting," Elena admitted, and Damon's smile widened. "But I should get to school. Aunt Judith will worry if she hears I cut."

"I could make her forget," Damon suggested, and held up a hand defensively when Elena glared at him. "Just teasing you, Princess. School it is."

Elena settled back in the soft leather of the passenger seat, and Damon shut the door behind her and crossed to the driver's side. She watched as he started the car and pulled out, admiring his strong, graceful hands on the wheel. When he shot her a sidelong smile, she grinned back. This was all so familiar. She knew the way he scanned the road, the way his long legs fit into the footwell of the car. *This is* Damon, she thought, with a sigh of satisfaction. When she was with him, she felt at home.

When they pulled into the parking lot at school, Caroline's head shot up first. All around her, their friends turned as if drawn by a single, invisible thread. Damon parked and got out, coming around the car to open Elena's door with a flourish.

"Who is *that*?" She heard Bonnie's voice rise above the crowd. Meredith shushed her.

She smiled prettily up at Damon as he helped her out of the car, pretending not to notice the spreading whispers all around them.

"They'll be talking about you all day," Damon said, his voice low. Elena gave him a small, private grin in reply.

"I'll see you later?" Elena asked him, squeezing his cool hand in her warmer one.

"Oh, I'll be around," he said, and bent his head to press his lips, lightly, against her cheek. Raising her hand to touch where he had kissed, Elena watched as Damon slid back into his car and drove away. A tendril of affection curled warmly inside her.

Once the black car had turned out of the high school parking lot, an excited babble of voices rose up behind Elena.

"Did you *see* that car?"

"There was a car? I was too busy looking at the *guy*."

"No wonder Elena didn't care about the new boy."

Elena smirked a little. Then, turning, she came face to face with Matt. His lips were pursed tightly. Elena flinched. She had told him there wasn't anyone else.

"Matt," she said quickly, "it's not what it looks like. When we talked, I didn't …"

Tyler Smallwood and Dick Carter swaggered over. Tyler slapped Matt on the back, his big, red face openly amused. "So someone finally cracked the Ice Princess, huh? Too bad it wasn't you, Honeycutt," he said loudly. "You wasted a lot of time there."

On Tyler's other side, Dick Carter broke into rough laughter. His girlfriend, Vickie Bennett, clung to his arm and tittered uneasily.

Ignoring them, Elena reached out for Matt. "I wasn't seeing Damon yet when we talked," she said. "I wouldn't lie to you."

"It's fine," Matt said shortly, turning away from her and heading for the school doors.

"Matt—" Elena began. She tried to follow him, but Tyler blocked her path, taking a firm hold on her arm.

"Tell you what, gorgeous," he said, baring his large white teeth in a smile. "Forget them both and come to Homecoming with me. We'll show you a good time, won't we, Dick? Vickie?"

Dick laughed, a big dumb har-de-har, and Elena squirmed away, pulling her arm out of Tyler's hot grip. "Forget it," she said briefly, but by the time she pushed past them, Matt was gone.

Tyler had always been a jerk, Elena thought dismissively. And then she felt her own eyes widen as what he had said hit her. Homecoming night.

Elena had been so *angry* that night. Angry at everyone: Stefan for snubbing her; Caroline for bringing Stefan to Homecoming; Bonnie and Meredith for thinking that perhaps she should give up on Stefan. And so she had drunk bourbon with Tyler and Dick and their friends, and gone with them to the cemetery.

Tyler had tried to rape Elena. Stefan had rescued her—that was the one moment that had torn down the barriers between them. *It doesn't matter*, Elena thought, repressing a shudder. That wasn't going to happen this time.

But Tyler and the others would probably still go to the cemetery. And Dick and Vickie had fooled around on Honoria Fell's tomb. The tomb that hid the entrance to the catacombs in which Katherine was concealed. Offended, Katherine had tormented Vickie for months, nearly driving her over the edge of insanity.

Elena glanced back at Vickie, who was now crossing the parking lot toward the school, still arm in arm with Dick. Vickie's pale brown hair flowed down her back as she tossed back her head to giggle up at Dick, her nose wrinkling as she laughed.

Elena had to try to protect her.

"Elena?" Bonnie's voice jolted Elena out of her contemplation. She was staring across at Tyler, she realized, frozen. She shook her head quickly, as if to scatter the memories, and turned to her friend.

Meredith was beside Bonnie, looking at Tyler with an expression of disdain. "Don't let him get to you, Elena," she said. "He's a creep."

"But who was that guy, Elena?" Bonnie demanded, her eyes shining with curiosity. "He was so—and you—Is *he* what you've been acting so weird about?"

"I'll tell you later," Elena said absently, watching as Vickie twisted a lock of her pale brown hair around one finger.

"Oh, come on!" Bonnie groaned, tugging at Elena's arm. "A beautiful guy like that? Tell me now!"

"I can't," Elena said, pulling away. "I promise I'll tell you everything I can soon. But right now we have to go to class." She would have to figure out *something* to tell them. Maybe she could pretend Damon was what he had told Aunt Judith, just a college student who Elena had happened to meet.

Bonnie huffed and rolled her eyes, but Meredith nodded. "Come on, then," she said. "We're going to be late."

Elena followed her friends toward the school doors, but her steps slowed as she saw Stefan waiting just outside, his face as gray as a storm cloud.

"I have to talk to you," he said, grabbing hold of her arm. Elena stared at him, and he let go, snatching his hand back. "Alone. Please."

Elena hesitated, and Meredith eyed her carefully. "Do you want us to go ahead without you?" she asked, ignoring Stefan.

"It's fine," Elena said with a grateful glance. Meredith nodded and tugged Bonnie after her into the school.

"Wait," Bonnie was saying, outraged. "I didn't think she even *knew* Stefan."

Elena watched her friends walk away before she looked up at Stefan, who had pulled off his sunglasses. His lips were drawn into a tight line.

"Elena," he said abruptly. "What do you know about that guy who drove you here?"

She should have realized this would happen. Unthinkingly, Elena raised a hand to touch Stefan, but he flinched back from her. "It's okay," she said steadily. "I know what I'm doing."

"I know you've got no reason to trust me," he told her. His eyes were dark, insisting. "But he's dangerous." He stepped closer, taking hold of her arm again, and his touch sent a hot spark through her.

"He's not dangerous to me," Elena said slowly, holding Stefan's eyes with her own.

"Do you remember me telling you that you reminded me of someone?" Stefan asked her. He was gripping Elena's arm so hard that it ached, and she held her breath. "Well, that girl died. And it was Damon's fault. Damon's and mine. He destroys everything he touches, and he doesn't care. You *have* to stay away from him." Stefan was breathing hard.

If only Elena could take Stefan in her arms and hold onto him, shut out the world so she could do nothing but bring Stefan comfort.

"I'm sorry, Stefan," she whispered, pulling her arm from his grip and brushing past him into the school. She could feel his eyes watching her. Elena didn't look back.

## 12

"But where did you even meet him?" Bonnie asked, rifling through a rack of dresses. "Ooh, pink. I think I might do pink for Homecoming this year." She pulled a fluffy concoction of satin and chiffon off the rack and held it up to herself to admire in the mirror. "Adorable, right?"

"It's cute," Elena agreed. "You should try it on." The three girls had headed right after school to one of their favorite boutiques to look for dresses for Homecoming.

Even as she flipped through the dresses, a little sore place deep in her chest kept reminding Elena that this might be the end. If she wasn't successful—if she *died*, back in that future—she would never be with her best friends again. And so she wanted, just for one afternoon, to be frivolous and try on dresses and talk about hairstyles.

"Focus, Bonnie," Meredith said, amused. "I'd like to know where Elena met him, too."

"At the cemetery, actually," Elena admitted, and Bonnie gasped, almost dropping the pink dress.

"You went back to the cemetery? Elena, they still haven't found who attacked that old man. It's not safe."

"I haven't been there since we promised Mary we'd stay away," Elena said patiently. "I met Damon before that."

Meredith's eyes narrowed. "The day we found you there?" At Elena's nod, she frowned. "So he was hanging out at the cemetery alone the day the old man was attacked?"

"So was I," Elena said dryly. "Damon has family buried there." She wasn't exactly lying, she told herself. Katherine, who had turned Damon into a vampire, was a kind of "family." And her lurking underground in the crypt could count as being "buried."

Bonnie rolled her eyes. "I really don't think Elena's gorgeous rich new boyfriend is attacking homeless people in his spare time, Meredith."

"Even gorgeous rich guys can be psychos," Meredith pointed out, her voice light.

"That may be true, but Damon's not one of them," she said, shortly. She began flipping through the rack of dresses in front of her and hesitated on a long sweep of silver silk. "This would look great on you, Meredith."

Meredith looked at it critically. "You don't think it's too plain? Or too long?"

"You can pull it off." Elena was sure the color would bring out her cool gray eyes and olive skin, while her natural elegance could carry off the style.

"So, are you bringing this Damon to the dance?" Bonnie asked.

"I don't think high school dances are really Damon's thing," Elena said. She had trouble imagining Damon slow dancing to pop songs and bringing her little cups of punch. And Stefan would be taking Caroline to the dance, she assumed. It was better for the Salvatore brothers not to be in the same room, especially not surrounded by humans.

"Who are you going to go with, then?" Bonnie asked, taking both the short pink dress and a blue green gown in a mermaid style off the rack to try on. "I'm sure Matt would still take you."

Elena shrugged. "No one, I guess."

Silently, Meredith and Bonnie turned to stare at Elena.

"What?" she asked, but she knew. The Elena who *belonged* here wouldn't be caught dead without a date for a school dance. She hadn't cared about any of those dates, either, not until Stefan.

"Are you actually going crazy?" Bonnie asked tartly, and then gasped as Meredith elbowed her in the side. "I mean, fine, great. Who needs a date anyway?"

"It's not a bad idea," Meredith said casually. "I was supposed to go with Ed Goff, but it might be more fun for us three to just go together. Not even bother with boys." There was something tentative to her gaze, and Elena realized what it was. Meredith was worried about her.

"Are you *both* crazy?" Bonnie asked. "I want to go with a boy. I want to dance all night. I want romance."

"With Raymond?" Meredith asked, arching an eyebrow. "There's nothing wrong with Raymond, but you can't pretend you're all that interested in him."

"I can pretend anything I want," Bonnie said, crossing her arms, the dresses she held crumpling against her.

"Come on, Bonnie," Elena said coaxingly. "If you go with us, you can dance with all the boys. And we'll have more fun together, you know we will."

"It's our last Homecoming together," Meredith said, laying her hand on Bonnie's arm. "It should be the three of us."

"Oh … oh … fine," Bonnie said. "But there had better be lots of cute boys who want to dance with me."

"Of course there will be," Meredith said reassuringly, "because you're going to look so great in one of these dresses."

"Obviously," said Bonnie with a suddenly teasing, crooked grin. She stuck her nose into the air and sailed off to the dressing room.

Meredith searched through the racks of dresses efficiently, pulling out a short jewel blue dress to add to the growing pile in her arms. Flicking past a green velvet minidress, Elena wished she could be so enthusiastic. Nothing seemed quite right.

"Here," Meredith said, stopping. "This is perfect for you."

The dress was gorgeous. Silk the color of crystallized violets, which would bring out the gold of her hair and the deep blue of her eyes. Elena would look magical in it, lit from within. *Had* looked magical.

It was what she had worn to the dance, the first time. Tyler had torn this dress. Stefan had fallen in love with her, finally taken her in his arms, while she was wearing it.

Elena stuffed her hands in her pockets, unwilling to touch it.

And then, she saw something on the other side of the room, just waiting for her. *Yes.* Elena brushed past Meredith and headed straight for it.

The iced-violet concoction was a beautiful dress. But this? This dress was a revelation.

It was red, the deep vibrant crimson of blood, and it would cling to Elena like a glove. Even hanging on the rack, it spoke of passion and intensity. It was a dress to fall in love in, or to stir up hate. If Damon were a dress, this was the one he would be.

"This is it," Elena breathed.

Meredith's eyebrows shot up. "Wow. It's a statement, all right."

They headed into the dressing room, Meredith with an armload of selections, Elena with only the crimson gown. Pulling it over her head, she called over the wall of the dressing room, "Want to get dressed for the dance at my place?"

"We always do," Bonnie called back.

It had been a ritual of theirs from their earliest dances in junior high to get dressed together, gossiping and doing one another's hair. Caroline had always been with them, but Elena didn't think she was going to join this time.

Elena smoothed the dress down over her hips and admired herself in the mirror. It fit perfectly, and the weight of the material—some kind of satin—made her feel powerful and protected.

"This is it," she said, stepping out of the fitting room. Meredith and Bonnie came out in dresses of their own.

"Wow," Bonnie said, looking Elena over. "I wouldn't have thought red was your color, but you look great. Older." She was in the mermaid green dress. "I don't love this one. I'm going to try on the gold."

Meredith looked sleek and composed in a black-and-gold dress with a long slit up the side, but she frowned. "This itches. Next!"

Elena changed back into her own clothes, draping the red dress carefully over her arm. *Caroline would have liked this dress*, she thought.

"Who's Caroline going with?" she asked. She couldn't help it; she had to know if she was going with Stefan again.

"I don't know," Meredith said. "She's been avoiding all of us."

"She never tells me anything anymore," Bonnie said. "If it weren't for math and history, I wouldn't see her at all." She sounded forlorn, and Elena had a pang of regret for the lost friendship. Maybe, now that they weren't competing over Stefan anymore, Caroline and Elena could be friends again, someday.

The fitting room doors opened again, and Elena stepped out to see the next set of dresses. An idea was kindling at the back of her mind. Why not replace Caroline in their little pre-dance group? It would be one way to keep the horrors of her first homecoming night from repeating. She thought of Vickie's innocent face, the way she had giggled at everything Dick said. How the walls of her room had been coated with blood in the future Elena had lived through. Things had to be different.

"Why don't we invite Vickie Bennett?" she said brightly. If Vickie was with them, she wouldn't leave the dance with Dick and Tyler. She wouldn't desecrate the tomb, wouldn't incite Katherine's anger.

Meredith, dressed in the long silver gown, and Bonnie, in black velvet, stared at her. "You want to invite Vickie Bennett?" Bonnie said slowly.

"Why not?" Elena asked. "What do you have against Vickie?"

Bonnie exchanged a glance with Meredith. Meredith cleared her throat. "Neither of us has a problem with Vickie, but *you've* never liked her."

Nodding, Bonnie added. "You've always said she was a useless little drip."

"Oh." A little twist of self-disgust curdled inside her. "Well, I was wrong. Let's bring her along."

After careful comparisons, Meredith chose the long silver gown, which looked like moonlight on her. Bonnie modeled fourteen different dresses and finally settled on the pink chiffon. Elena, of course, bought the red dress.

Leaving the store, she held her head high, feeling like a warrior. Like a hero. Elena wasn't *just* going to save Damon and herself. She would save everyone.

# 13

The weather Friday evening couldn't have been more perfect for the Homecoming game. Gold and pink from the setting sun striped the sky. On the field, the marching band stepped in precise formation for their pregame show, horns blaring and drums thumping. Cheerleaders cartwheeled in their red and black skirts, warming up the crowd for the game.

"The Homecoming game is a real American tradition," Elena told Damon, leading him up the bleachers. "You owe it to yourself to experience it at least once. I can't believe you've never been."

"You'd be amazed at the number of real American traditions I've been able to avoid," Damon said dryly.

"Well," Elena said, sitting down and wrapping her jacket more closely around her, "I'm glad I get a chance to introduce you to something."

Damon reached out and tucked a lock of Elena's hair behind her ear. "You're going to show me life in the light, right, Princess?" he asked, his voice low and teasing. "Football games and sock hops?"

"I don't think sock hops are a thing anymore, Damon," Elena told him, letting her voice take on a flirtatious edge. The brush of his fingers made her skin tingle. Sensing her reaction, Damon smiled and ran his hand down her arm, wrapping his fingers around hers.

This wasn't *her* Damon, not yet, but he felt so familiar that she kept forgetting. The weight of his arm across her shoulders, the scent of his leather jacket, the cool skin of his wrist resting casually against her neck, the affection that shone through his mocking smile: It all belonged to her Damon, too.

Elena could feel eyes watching them from all around as they sat waiting for the game to begin. Elena Gilbert with a mysterious, shockingly handsome, older man. Gossip would center on this for days.

No one approached them, though. Elena saw Meredith and Bonnie climbing the bleachers, Bonnie's face brightening as she saw them, and sent a silent plea to Meredith with her eyes. Meredith cocked one elegant eyebrow— message received—and shepherded Bonnie toward a group of laughing girls in another row of seats.

As the team ran out onto the field to claps and cheers, Damon tensed beside her, letting go of Elena's hand.

His jaw was tight, and his eyes followed one red-and-black jersey across the field. Stefan.

She was surprised to see Stefan on the team. Perhaps she should have realized that, even without her intercession, Matt would have invited Stefan to try out for the team.

"My appreciation for football is fading," Damon said dryly, his eyes still fixed on Stefan. "Let's go somewhere else, Princess. I can show you all kinds of things better than high school sports." He turned toward her, his lips twitching up in a wicked smile, and took her hand again, starting to rise.

"No, wait, Damon," Elena said quickly, tugging him back down. "I need a favor."

Damon's eyes narrowed. Slowly, he sat back in his seat and fixed her with a steady dark gaze. "So you didn't just want to expand my horizons when you brought me here?" He leaned closer. "You're quite devious, aren't you, Elena?"

Pulling her eyes away from his, Elena looked back at the field. Their team had won the coin flip, and Matt, as quarterback and captain, chose to receive the kickoff. The teams were lining up, and Elena gripped Damon's hand harder as she leaned forward to scan the backs of their jerseys. "See those two guys?" she said, pointing. "Carter and Smallwood."

Damon glanced at them, his face taking on the thoughtful look she associated with him using his Power. "A couple of all-American meatheads," he said dismissively. "Nothing special about them."

"I know," Elena said. "I need them to fight. It has to be bad enough to get them kicked off the team."

Damon's eyebrows rose. "You're more bloodthirsty than I'd realized, Princess," he said.

"I need them to get suspended. They can't be at the dance tomorrow," Elena told him. The kicker was moving back, his teammates lined up on either side. "*Please*, Damon," she said.

Damon leaned back and smiled lazily at her. "Why should I?" His eyes were locked on hers, challenging her. "What will you give me?"

"Anything you want," Elena said recklessly. "I trust you. Just do it."

Damon's smile widened, and he flicked his eyes back toward the field. The kicker's foot made contact with the ball, and it flew in a high arc through the air.

With a shout of fury, Tyler Smallwood launched himself across the field and tackled Dick Carter to the ground.

The stands broke out in screaming excitement. Tyler was punching Dick in the stomach, avoiding his pads to reach the flesh beneath. Dick bucked and rolled, and Tyler hit the ground with a thud.

"Good enough?" Damon asked.

Down on the field, the referees were blowing hard on their whistles and running toward the fight. Both boys had pulled off their helmets, and, as Elena watched, Dick punched Tyler hard in the nose. Bright blood gushed out, drops spilling onto the grass of the football field.

"That should do it," Elena said, feeling a little sick. But this was necessary. If Tyler and Dick went to the dance, if they left the dance and went to the graveyard, terrible things would happen.

This was the better option.

The coaches were shouting as the other players tried unsuccessfully to pull Dick and Tyler apart. Tyler lunged forward and sank his teeth into Dick's arm. There was more blood, running over Tyler's mouth. Damon was watching, his face lit with pleasure.

"Damon!" Elena said sharply. "That's enough!"

"Killjoy," Damon muttered, but he glared at the fighting boys, and they stilled, then pulled away from each other. Matt and one of the running backs were holding onto them, tugging them farther apart. Both boys looked dazed, and Tyler wiped at his mouth, smearing dark red blood across his face.

A chill spread through Elena. The pleasure Damon took in watching the guys fight was something she hadn't seen in years. As comfortable as she felt with him, she still needed to be careful.

Down on the field, Stefan was paying no attention to the aftermath of the fight going on all around him. Instead, he was scanning the stands, his eyes narrowed. He must be looking for Damon, Elena realized. Of course Stefan would suspect Damon was behind the fight.

Before Stefan could spot them, the referees called the teams back into place. Two second-string players ran out to take Tyler and Dick's places, and the game began at last.

Elena was surprised at how much she enjoyed it. She had been to football games before, of course she had. But usually, what was going on in the stands had interested her more than what might be happening on the field. Even when she was dating Matt, she hadn't really *watched* him play.

He was really good. Matt and Stefan made an incredible team, but Stefan had the strength, speed, and reflexes of a vampire. Matt was managing on pure skill. Calm and confident, he called the plays, his eyes scanning the field. He ran like the wind, and when he passed the ball downfield, it was in a long spiraling arc that landed safely in Stefan's hands. No wonder he had been—was going to be—offered football scholarships.

Damon watched the crowd far more than he did the game, although his eyes regularly flitted back to Stefan. When he looked at his brother, he wore an expression that

Elena couldn't quite decipher. Was this hostile face the one Damon had worn all those centuries, as he kept a distant eye on his little brother, his enemy?

At halftime, Damon bought Elena a cup of hot chocolate.

"Thank you," she said, pleased at his thoughtfulness, and wrapped her fingers around the warmth of the cup. It was getting chilly. Fall had really set in now.

"May I?" Damon asked politely, after he'd watched her take a sip. She handed over the hot chocolate, and he drank slowly, savoring. "Very nice," he said. "Sweet." His fingers lingered on hers for a moment longer than necessary as he passed the cup back to her. Damon's words were innocent enough, but there was something darkly teasing in his gaze. Attraction hummed between them. Maybe he wasn't her Damon yet, but he *would* be.

\* \* \*

When they got back to Elena's house after the game, the driveway was empty.

"Aunt Judith must have taken Margaret somewhere," Elena told Damon.

Damon tipped his head slightly to one side, clearly sending out his Power to search the house. "There's no one home."

"*Mmmhmm.*" Elena unlocked the door and stepped inside. Damon waited on the porch, his hands in his jacket pockets, casual and confident. Elena didn't hesitate. If she wanted Damon to be trustworthy, first she had to trust him. "You can come in if you want," she said. "The invitation still stands."

"If you want me," Damon said cooly, but there was a pleased tilt to his mouth as he followed her in.

Elena led Damon through the house. In the hall, he paused, running his fingers across the photographs on the side table. "Your mother?" he asked, picking one up to look at it more closely.

Elena nodded, her throat tight. Damon kept touching things as he followed her through the house, brushing his fingers over the furniture and opening drawers to look inside. Up in her room, he prowled like a cat, inspecting the books on Elena's bookcase, rifling through the clothes in her closet, delicately rearranging the objects on her dresser. It was as if he was trying to figure her out.

Finally, he put down her silver comb and turned to look at her. "Why did you want them to fight?" he asked, his voice dry. "It's not for love, is it?"

Elena laughed in spite of herself. "Tyler or Dick? Absolutely not." Sobering, she added, "I know something terrible would have happened tomorrow if they hadn't been suspended. I can't explain any more. I'm sorry."

Damon stepped closer and brought his hands up to frame her face. His eyes, so dark that she couldn't distinguish the iris from the pupil, stared into hers. Electricity shot through her at the careful touch of Damon's hands on her face. He was trying to use his Power to read her, she could tell.

"You're not a witch," he said, confidently. "Or a psychic."

Elena reached up and took his cool hands in hers. "Like I told you, I'm just a girl who knows some things. I'm nothing special."

"I wouldn't say that," Damon said, turning his palm so that his fingers were interlaced with hers. His eyes followed the line of the vein in her neck, all the way down to the collar of her shirt. "You promised me anything I wanted," he said.

He expected her to pull away, to be afraid, Elena knew. Instead, she brushed her hair back, cocking her head to expose the smooth line of her throat. "I trust you," she said simply.

Damon stared for a moment, then pulled her closer, wrapping his arms around her, and kissed her throat. Beneath the softness of his lips, his sharp canines pricked her, and she pressed closer still. *Yes.*

When his teeth slid smoothly beneath her skin, she could feel Damon with her at last: all his anger and loneliness, that lost child she knew hid beneath his cold façade.

And, deeper still, passion. Love that never ended, a burn-ing fire that could never be extinguished.

Their minds intertwined, and Elena stifled a sob of pure joy. Damon was hers again. They were both going to live.

#TVD13LovingDelena

## 14

"They were both amazing," Bonnie said from the window seat. She was already wearing her fluffy pink dress, her bouncy curls perfectly smooth.

"Who?" Elena murmured as Meredith twisted a long strand of her hair and secured it with a bobby pin.

"Matt and Stefan," Bonnie said. "When Stefan caught that last pass, I thought I was going to faint. Or throw up."

"Oh, *please*," said Meredith.

Vickie Bennett, carefully ringing her eyes with liner in front of the mirror, giggled nervously. She'd been thrilled when Elena invited her to join them in getting ready for the dance, but she seemed hesitant and unsure now that she was there. As Elena watched, Vickie glanced quickly at her, then looked away, her free hand twisting the hem of her dress.

"And Matt—that boy is simply poetry in motion …" Bonnie wriggled around on the seat to fix a bright eye on Elena. "You could have gotten either of them to take you, you know. Matt's still crazy about you. And he's a sweetheart. Plus, I saw Stefan's face after Damon brought you to school. He practically swallowed his tongue, he was so upset."

"It doesn't matter," Elena said. "I'm with Damon."

"Then why isn't he bringing you to the dance?" Meredith asked, her talented fingers twining more of Elena's hair into an elegant golden mass. "Even if he doesn't like dances, he should have come if you wanted him to."

"But I didn't want him to," Elena said, laughing and catching Meredith's hand as she tweaked another strand of Elena's hair into place. "I wanted to go with you guys."

Bonnie sat up straighter, her small face growing serious. "I'm glad you did, Elena," she said. "Remember how I saw in your palm that you had two loves? I think … I think something bad might happen if you aren't careful."

Meredith huffed out an exasperated breath. "Bonnie—"

"I just mean," Bonnie said, "that if she wants Damon, it doesn't matter that Matt and Stefan like her. That's all. Two loves aren't necessarily better than one. You need to be careful, Elena."

"And you should leave some guys for the rest of us," Meredith said lightly. Bonnie laughed and looked away, but Elena shifted uneasily under Meredith's hands. How much of the future could Bonnie see? And which future was it?

It didn't matter. Elena knew what would happen tonight. Caroline and Stefan would be at the dance together. Elena would leave them alone this time. She wouldn't ask Stefan to dance. Caroline, Elena thought, would have a perfectly nice time. There wasn't going to be a second love for Elena this time. Whatever Bonnie saw, it wasn't going to happen.

"It's fun to go with just girls, anyway," Meredith said. "You were right, Elena."

"Sure," Bonnie said, rolling her eyes. "Guys: Who needs them?"

Vickie turned away from the mirror to face them and said, in an awkward rush, "Thanks for inviting me to come with you. I probably wouldn't have gone at all otherwise."

"What happened with Dick and Tyler, anyway?" Bonnie asked curiously. "Did Dick tell you what they were fighting about?"

Vickie spread her hands wide, shrugging in amazement. "All Dick is said was that suddenly he was so angry he couldn't even see straight. The next thing he knew, everybody was pulling him and Tyler apart."

Meredith frowned. "They don't take steroids, do they?"

"No! I don't think so." Vickie was shaking her head, but a shadow of doubt crept into her voice.

Again, Elena felt a flicker of guilt. She remembered the way Dick's head had snapped backward when Tyler punched him in the mouth, the dazed expressions on both their faces when the other players had finally pulled them apart.

But worse things would have happened if they had gone to the church that night. Stefan had almost killed Dick and Tyler after Elena drowned. Vickie had been gruesomely murdered. The memory of Vickie's room, painted in blood, made Elena's stomach turn over.

What were a few rumors or a suspension to that?

"There," Meredith slid the last bobby pin into Elena's hair. "Gorgeous."

Elena stood and pulled her friends close so that they could all look in the mirror. Bonnie, her curls falling over her shoulders, was as sweet as candy in her shimmering pink taffeta. Meredith's hair was swept up into an elegant chignon, and the long sweep of silver silk falling almost to her feet made her seem a thousand times more sophisticated than she'd ever seemed before. Even Vickie, in a soft green dress that came to her knees and ended in a puff of lace, looked fresh and delicate despite her nervousness.

As for herself, Elena thought, standing straight and tall in the crimson dress, she looked like a burning flame. She looked like she could set the world on fire.

They walked down the stairs together to where Aunt Judith and her fiancé, Robert, waited, along with pajama-clad Margaret. Margaret jumped to her feet and came to hug Elena around the waist. Elena bent down and kissed her little sister on the forehead.

Aunt Judith blinked when she saw Elena. "You girls all look lovely," she said slowly. "That's certainly a ... dramatic dress, dear."

"You're pretty," Margaret said, beaming up at Elena, and Elena gave her a squeeze.

"Runs in the family," she whispered, and her little sister giggled.

Robert was staring at Elena, looking a little dazed.

"What's the matter, Bob?" Aunt Judith asked.

"Oh." He frowned and passed a hand across his forehead. "Actually, it just occurred to me that *Elena* is a form of the name *Helen*. And for some reason I was thinking of Helen of Troy."

"Beautiful and doomed," said Bonnie. Her eyes met Elena's for a second, before she quickly looked away.

"Well, yes," said Robert.

A chill went up Elena's spine. She *wasn't* doomed, she told herself fiercely. Not this time. There was nothing to worry about. "We have to go," she said quickly, and kissed Aunt Judith good-bye. "Don't wait up."

They all rode to the dance together in Meredith's car, Elena in the front passenger seat, Bonnie and Vickie in the back. Meredith and Vickie were laughing and chattering, and Elena tried to join in.

But Bonnie was oddly quiet, and when Elena looked into the backseat, the other girl's brown eyes were fixed on her thoughtfully. Elena couldn't escape the heavy, anxious feeling that something important, something terrible, was about to happen.

*No,* she told herself. *It's just a high school dance. I'm only afraid because of what happened the first time. Everything is different now.* But the thoughts didn't lighten the sickening feeling of dread at the bottom of Elena's stomach.

She almost leaned over and asked Meredith to take her home. She could have given some excuse, said she felt ill—it wouldn't even have been a lie. But she was Elena Gilbert, and she did not back down. She would hold her head high and enjoy this last dance. There was nothing to be afraid of.

\* \* \*

Music spilled out the open doors of the auditorium as they arrived. Inside, the cavernous room was a swirling mass of people, laughter, and voices. The decoration committee had draped the walls in long swathes of sheer fabric that shone gently in the light, transforming the whole auditorium into something from a dream. In the center of everything, resplendent in gold, was Caroline.

"Look at that dress," Bonnie said, softly. "What's the front held on with? Superglue?"

The dazzling dress, made of gold lamé and fitting like a second skin, certainly showed a lot of Caroline. She looked beautiful and wild, her glossy auburn hair streaming down her back as she laughed. Her long limbs were smooth and tanned, and her cat-green eyes shone. Caroline was clearly having a wonderful time.

Elena looked for Stefan beside Caroline, but she couldn't spot him. The crowd around Caroline was constantly shifting. People came up to speak to her briefly, admiringly, like courtiers to a queen, and then stepped back to make room for the next in line.

"Born to rule, apparently," Meredith said, sounding amused.

Elena kept moving toward Caroline, scanning the changing crowd around her. Stefan had to be there somewhere. Elena wouldn't speak to him, wouldn't touch him, but she wanted to *see* him. She could have that at least, surely?

As a couple of cheerleaders stepped aside, Elena saw Caroline's date at last and stopped short for a second in surprise.

Not Stefan at all. Matt. His hand was resting lightly on Caroline's arm as he stood beside her, prince consort to the queen, but his eyes were fixed on Elena, his jaw set defiantly.

Elena held her head high and started walking toward them again, fixing a smile on her face. She didn't own

Matt. She'd prepared herself, she thought, to see Stefan with Caroline. She wasn't ready, though, for the sharp sense of loss at seeing Matt with her instead. Elena hadn't quite realized how much she thought of Matt as *belonging* to her, at least in this time. Beyond her feeling possessive of him, Caroline couldn't possibly be good for Matt.

Vickie had wandered off toward the refreshment table, and Meredith and Bonnie, one after the other, were asked to dance and went off onto the dance floor.

"Hey, Elena. Want to dance?" It was her lab partner, a tall, gangly guy with a wicked sense of humor who normally she'd have enjoyed dancing with. But Elena just shook her head, barely glancing at him.

"Not yet," she said shortly. "I need to talk to somebody. I'll catch up with you later."

As Elena reached the outskirts of the group around her, Caroline looked up and their eyes met. Elena smiled, but Caroline just gazed at her. And then she smiled, and, turning toward Matt, tipped her face up to his and kissed him, a long passionate kiss.

Elena felt her own face drawing into a scowl and consciously smoothed it over, fixing a neutral, almost bored expression in its place.

"Hello, Elena," Caroline drawled, as soon as the kiss ended. "Don't you look"—her eyes flicked over the crimson dress—"nice. It's so original of you to wear that shade of red with your complexion. A lot of people would worry about looking washed out."

Elena forced a smile. "Hello, Caroline. Hello, Matt."

Up on the stage near them, the principal tapped his finger against the microphone, clearing his throat. "Can I get the Homecoming Court up on stage, please? It's time to crown your queen!"

The crowd cheered, but Elena was hardly listening. Instead, she was looking beyond Caroline and Matt. She was positive that Stefan was here, somewhere in the crowd. Even if he hadn't brought Caroline, surely he had come.

The crowd was shifting around her as the princesses, Bonnie and Meredith among them, climbed the steps to the stage. Elena turned her back on them for a minute, scanning the faces behind her for Stefan.

Then strong fingers, their pointed nails digging into her arm, dragged Elena back to attention. Caroline, eyes blazing, leaned in close as Elena pulled away.

"How does it feel, Elena?" she whispered, her voice hard. "How does it feel to know I've taken everything you wanted?" Almost stomping her feet, she swung around in a sweep of gold and auburn, and climbed the steps onto the stage, holding her head high.

Elena cocked a cynical eyebrow at Matt. "Caroline Forbes? Really?"

Matt's cheeks reddened and he looked away. "*You* broke up with *me*, Elena. I'll date who I want."

"Oh, Matt," Elena said, softening. She thought again of Jasmine, of the beautiful, smart, compassionate woman who would fall in love with Matt, who would hold on to him through all the dangers his life threw at them. "I *know* you can do better. Don't waste yourself on someone who just wants you as a trophy."

Matt sighed. "At least she wants me."

The principal had finished introducing each girl. Now he tore open an envelope. "And your new Homecoming Queen is Caroline Forbes!" Around them, the crowd cheered.

Elena squeezed Matt's hand. "I know you, Matt," she said in a quick, fierce whisper. "You don't take the easy route. You're not going to be happy unless a relationship is real, unless it's *true*. I'm sorry it's not going to be with me, but you don't have to settle. Promise me you're going to be ready, when that great girl shows up. Don't waste your time on the wrong people."

The principal lifted the shiny, plastic crown and placed it carefully on Caroline's head.

For the first time, Matt looked up and made real eye contact with Elena. There was a little bit of warmth in his eyes now, and his mouth turned up into a half smile. "Yeah, maybe," he said. "One of these days."

Caroline's eyes were shining, and she gripped her plastic scepter as if it were made of pure gold. Elena leaned forward and hugged Matt.

And then, behind Matt, she finally saw Stefan. With a satisfying sense of something slotting into place at last, her eyes locked with his. *This*, she thought, *all this time, I've been waiting for this.*

They were in a crowd of people, and his eyes were only on her. Just for now, couldn't she at least pretend he was hers?

tefan looked *perfect*. Under the dim auditorium lights, Stefan seemed so poised and handsome, his black blazer somehow better cut, more sophisticated than the other boys'. Elena couldn't make out the color of his eyes, not from this far away, but she knew how green they were, and how, with his sunglasses finally stripped away, they must be broadcasting every emotion he felt.

Elena's chest tightened as raw longing shot through her. She suddenly felt like she was suffocating, the noise and heat of people pressing in around her. She sucked in a desperate gasp of air.

Stefan's eyes were fixed on hers as he began to make his way toward her through the crowd. Elena's heart fluttered in her chest. *No.* She wasn't even allowed to pretend.

The connection between her and Stefan could kill them both.

"I have to go," she muttered, and let go of Matt.

"Elena?" Matt called, but she was already turning on her heel and walking away, as fast as she could without actually running. *Stay calm*, she ordered herself, but she was panting, unable to catch her breath. She hit the swinging door hard and found herself out in the brightly lit, almost empty halls of the school.

Elena leaned against the cool metal of the row of lockers across from the door of the auditorium, and closed her eyes for a moment.

She was never going to have Stefan again. All those years together, all they'd been through, and she couldn't even talk to him. All their history, wiped out. If she succeeded, it would never happen.

"Elena?" She knew that voice. Her eyes snapped open.

Stefan stood in front of her, his face soft with concern. "I heard what Caroline said to you," he said. "Are you all right?"

Elena couldn't help laughing, a short, almost-sob of a laugh. "You think I'm upset about *Caroline?*" she asked. It was so far-off it was as if Stefan didn't know her at all. *Well, he doesn't, not now*, she thought, and the thought cut off her laugh. Sobering, she snapped, "Whatever she thinks, I don't want anything Caroline has."

Stefan touched her cheek, gently drawing her gaze back to his, and a spark of electricity flew beneath Elena's skin at his touch. "I know that," he said. "I know you don't care about all this. Popularity. Dances. I've watched you, Elena, and I can tell you're not thinking about those things. But I also know that you're *sad*."

"Oh." Tears stung the backs of Elena's eyes, and she squeezed them tightly closed again, shaking her head. "Caroline's wrong about—well, almost everything. But, even if I don't want to be queen or date Matt, it's true that I can't have everything I want. And that hurts."

"Maybe ..." Stefan began, but his voice trailed off as Elena shook her head again, her mouth tight. She'd tried having everything, having both of the vampires she loved, more than once. It had taken her years to learn that trying to have both Damon and Stefan led to nothing but misery for all of them. She couldn't start down that road again, no matter how much she wanted to.

Stefan's oak-leaf green eyes were warm with sympathy, and his voice was soft. "I understand, Elena. I can't have the thing I want most either."

Elena couldn't help it. She leaned into his body, just a little, and Stefan's arms circled around her. Elena pressed her face against his shoulder. It was *Stefan*, Stefan who she'd missed so much.

Stefan let her cry, holding her while she shook for a few moments. Swallowing hard, Elena straightened up, her face back under control. Stefan's arms were still around her, as if he didn't want to let go.

"Sorry," she said, sniffing. "You must think I'm a lunatic."

"Not at all," Stefan said. He stroked her back gently, and Elena arched into his touch. "Shall we dance?"

"What?" Elena blinked in surprise. Music was streaming softly through the closed door from the auditorium. Stefan slowly lifted Elena's arms and twined them around his neck, then wrapped his own arms around her waist.

"We can't have what we want," he said with a note of longing in his voice. "But we could dance, just for now. It is a dance, after all."

They began to sway in time to the music, and Elena leaned her head against the delicate fabric of Stefan's blazer. His strong hands were holding her so tenderly, and she knew that he was looking down at her with painful, aching love shining through his face, now that he knew she couldn't see him.

Stefan was drawn to her, had wanted and needed her from the very beginning. This was one thing Elena knew, one thing that had always been true between them. But he would let her go without a word, for her own good. To keep Elena safe.

Elena was swept up in a great wave of emotion, of love and pity and passion, all mixed together. This was *Stefan.* How could she turn away from him, even for Damon?

Winding her arms around Stefan's neck, his soft brown curls brushing against her fingers, Elena pulled back a little and looked up into his face. His eyes were dilated with passion, the black expanding across the green.

What if Elena's plan didn't work? What if, no matter how she tried, Damon was fated to kill Mr. Tanner Halloween night? Or worse, what if she gave up Stefan, undid their love, for *nothing*?

Elena pulled him closer. Stefan's lips parted in surprise, and then, with an anguished look of surrender, he bent his head to hers. "What are you?" he murmured against her lips. "What is it about you?"

As their lips met, heat rushed through Elena's body. It felt so familiar, so right. Her Stefan. The rest of the world fell away.

Until a door burst open behind them.

*"Elena?"*

# 16

lena pulled out of Stefan's arms in a panic, stumbling backward as she put distance between them. What had she been *thinking*?

"Damon," she said as she turned to face him. Her heart was hammering hard, and she knew her voice sounded strained. "This isn't what it looks like."

Against the deadly pale of his skin, Damon's eyes blazed like black stars. In an instant, his face smoothly fell back into its customary detached irony. If Elena hadn't seen that momentary look of pain, she might have thought that there was a chance he'd listen to what she had to say.

Damon's lips tightened. "Funnily enough, I think it's exactly what it looks like, Elena," he said cooly. "My little brother makes a habit of trespassing on my territory." His eyes shifted, and then he was looking past Elena, as if she didn't matter, straight at Stefan. Stefan glared back, his jaw set stubbornly.

"As for you? I'll make you suffer," Damon told him, his voice cold and clear, ringing through the deserted hallway. "I told you I would kill you one day, and I will, but first I'm going to destroy everything you care about. You'll *beg* for death in the end." He flashed a brilliant, scornful smile with no humor in it at all. Faster than Elena's eye could follow, he was gone.

"*Damon!*" Elena tried to scream after him, but her voice was thin with shock, and it came out more a squeak than anything else.

She'd been such a fool, giving in to her emotions, and now she had ruined *everything*.

Elena forced herself still and took a deep gulp of air. Maybe there was time to salvage this. If she could find Damon, if she could explain ... Elena peered down the hall toward the shadowy corridors leading to the rest of the school. Where would Damon have gone? With a pang, she realized that she didn't know where he was living, had never known that sort of detail about this time in his life.

"Elena." In her moment of panic, she'd almost forgotten about Stefan. He gripped her by the arm, his voice low and urgent. "You need to get out of here. Find your friends and go somewhere safe, a house where Damon's never been. Take the flowers I gave you. If Damon comes to you, whatever you do, whatever he says, *don't let him in*."

Elena grabbed hold of Stefan's hand. "I just need to talk to Damon."

"It won't help," he said grimly. "Do what I told you, Elena, please."

And, in the moments between one blink and another, he was gone, too.

Elena swore, slamming her hand against a locker. Stefan was the *last* person who should be going after Damon now, and he ought to know that. But maybe he didn't care.

She took a deep breath and let it out slowly, then another, trying to calm her pounding heart.

Maybe Damon would go to Stefan's boardinghouse, looking for revenge. Or maybe she could figure out where he was staying. Damon liked luxury—she could check the nice hotel downtown and search for upscale, uninhabited houses. Inhabited ones, too. He had hidden her in an attic once, Elena remembered. She let out a long, frustrated sigh.

Damon could be anywhere. But maybe, just maybe … Elena looked up and down the halls at the banners cheering on the football team, the dented lockers. Damon had never been one to run away from conflict. He could still be in the school.

And if so, Elena needed to find him, fast.

Elena headed back into the auditorium, music and chatter swelling around her as she passed through the door. She waited for her eyes to adjust to the darkness as she scanned the crowd, trying to spot her friends.

She saw Meredith first, on the dance floor with a boy whose name Elena didn't know. Elena cut straight through the crowd toward them, putting her hand on Meredith's shoulder.

"I need your help. Please," she said.

Meredith took one glance at her and nodded. "I'll be back," she said to her partner with a smile, and tugged Elena to the side of the dance floor, whispering, "What? What's happened?"

"Let me get Bonnie and Matt first, and then I'll explain." Elena had spotted Bonnie, deeper in the crowd on the dance floor. She was dancing with Raymond and getting into the music, her eyes closed and her hands up in the air above her head. Elena shouldered her way toward her, ignoring the grumbles as she shoved past people.

"Bonnie. Come with us."

Bonnie opened her eyes and scowled. "I'm *dancing*," she said, without stopping.

"This is important." Elena tried to put all the anxiety she was feeling into her face.

Bonnie sighed and rolled her eyes at Raymond. "Girl stuff," she said. "I'll catch up with you later."

"Seriously, what's going on? It couldn't wait?" she hissed at Elena as they reached the edge of the dance floor and the crowd thinned out a little.

Over at the refreshment table, Matt was pouring two cups of punch. Elena headed for him, Bonnie and Meredith trailing behind her. "I need help finding Damon," Elena said. "He's here, and he saw me kissing Stefan."

Matt's eyebrows shot up his forehead, and Bonnie and Meredith exchanged a confused glance.

"You were kissing *Stefan?*" Bonnie asked, in a tone midway between scandalized and intrigued.

"I'm not sure this qualifies as an emergency," Meredith said dryly. "Maybe you should let him cool off and call him tomorrow."

Matt remained quiet, not able to look Elena in the eye.

Elena felt sick. Of course they weren't panicking. As far as the three of them were concerned, Damon was just a guy she was dating, and Stefan was a guy who went to their school. Good-looking, intense, mysterious guys, but, when you came right down to it, only human beings. They didn't understand how dangerous Damon—*this* Damon, the Damon of now—could be.

"This isn't going to be okay!" she said, hearing her own voice wobble wildly.

"Oh, Elena—" At her outburst, Bonnie's eyes widened in sympathy, and she wrapped her arms around Elena. "We'll help, whatever you need." She looked fiercely at Meredith and Matt, as if daring them to disagree. Meredith nodded in agreement, but Matt hesitated.

"I just—Caroline's waiting for me," he said, gazing down at the two cups of punch he was still clutching.

"Go ahead and take them to her and then come help us," Meredith said firmly.

"Caroline will get over it," Bonnie added, a smirk playing around the edges of her mouth.

Matt looked torn for a moment, and then his face firmed, his mind made up. "I'll be back," he said grimly, and marched off.

The three girls watched as he crossed the auditorium to where Caroline stood. At first, she smiled at Matt and accepted the cup of punch gracefully, as poised as a princess. Matt dipped his head to speak in her ear and, as she listened, Caroline's expression grew more and more thunderous. She snapped something back at him, and Matt replied. Then Caroline, clearly incandescent with rage, reared back and slapped Matt hard across the face.

"Oh my God," Bonnie breathed.

Matt swung around and hurried back to them. "I guess that's that" was all he said. There was a red mark high on his cheekbone where Caroline had slapped him.

Elena slipped her hand into his big, warm one and squeezed, just for a second. "Thank you." She didn't deserve him; she knew that.

As she let go, Matt looked down at her, shaking his head slightly from side to side. "I don't know why I do the things I do for you, Elena Gilbert," he said, but a rueful smile was beginning to tug at the corners of his mouth.

"Someday, I hope to return the favor," Elena said, then turned to her other friends. "If we split up, we can search the school more quickly." They pushed through the auditorium doors into the hall again. "But if you see Damon, just come get me, don't try talking to him. He's upset. If you see Stefan, try to get him to come back here."

"So Stefan went after Damon?" Meredith asked, confused. "Why? Do they even know each other?"

"They're brothers, but they don't get along very well," Elena told her.

She dug into the tiny lipstick-red purse she carried. It didn't hold a lot—just essentials—but one thing in here might be crucial. "Here." She pulled out the withered bunch of vervain, now looking more like a bunch of wilted, dead weeds than ever, and quickly divided it into four small portions, a few strands of vervain in each.

"Um, why are you giving us dead plants?" Bonnie asked, holding hers doubtfully between her thumb and forefinger, her nose wrinkling.

"They're good luck," Elena said, aware of how lame she sounded. "Damon's very superstitious."

They all stared at her but, with a shrug, Matt put his bunch into his suit jacket, and Meredith into her clutch. Bonnie, purseless, tucked them behind her ear.

They split up, Matt and Bonnie heading down the hall toward the cafeteria, Meredith and Elena going the other way toward the office. As they walked, Elena glanced into every dim classroom, checking for Damon or Stefan.

"Maybe you should just let Damon calm down on his own," Meredith said hesitantly, but Elena shook her head.

"I have to find him." The longer she and Meredith looked, the more urgently Elena felt that time was running out. She knew Damon was only getting angrier by the minute.

Unease spread inside Elena, the feeling that someone was watching her from the shadows. The skin on the back of her neck crawled. She stopped to listen.

In the distance, someone laughed, and quick footsteps ran down a nearby hallway. Probably just another student, someone ducking out of the dance. Elena took a deep breath and pushed open the next classroom door. No one.

"Do you really think—" Meredith began. She broke off as the fire alarm suddenly began to blare, a deafening screech. Despite herself, Elena jumped.

"Some kid always has to set it off and try to ruin everyone's good time," Meredith half shouted over the alarm, disgusted.

Elena shook her head. She could smell smoke, faint and faraway for now, but there. "I don't think so," she said. In the distance, she could hear frantic shouts, the principal's voice rising over the loudspeakers, directing everyone out of the building.

It was a real fire, she was sure of it. She was also sure that Damon had started it. Elena looked around wildly, searching for some clue to his whereabouts.

"Over here," she said, picking a direction and hurrying forward. They hadn't looked in the theater yet, maybe Damon—or Stefan—was there.

The smoke grew thicker as they made their way deeper into the school. "Elena, stop!" Meredith called, her heels clicking against the floor as she ran after Elena.

"I'm sure he's down here," Elena called back. Damon would want to see the chaos he had created. She could picture him, flames reflected in his dark eyes.

Meredith caught up to her, grabbing hold of Elena's arm with strong fingers. "It's not safe," she said. "We have to get out of here."

Meredith dragged Elena around the corner, but they were faced with a searing wave of heat. Flames licked the ceiling, melting the lockers like they were made of candle wax. Both girls shrieked as the fire crackled and grew.

"I need to find him," Elena said, sobs beginning to rise in her throat, her eyes stinging from the smoke.

But, as Meredith took began to pull her toward the fire exit, Elena felt suddenly, horrifyingly sure that she was too late. She'd lost Damon. She'd failed.

## 17

The windows of the school glowed red as flames within climbed the walls, reaching for the upper floors. The bricks of its façade were cracking in the heat. As Elena and her friends watched from the parking lot, a window shattered.

"Oh my God," Bonnie said softly. The reflected flames made her pale face rosy. Next to her, Meredith leaned her head on Matt's shoulder, gazing wide-eyed into the flames.

It seemed like the teachers had gotten everyone out of the dance, smoke-smeared and disheveled in the remains of their formal clothes. Near Elena's group, a girl sobbed hysterically, long streaks of soot crossing her face, while farther away, one of the football players hacked dryly, a casualty of the smoke.

Only a few minutes after Meredith and Elena had reached the parking lot, the fire trucks pulled in, sirens screaming. But by that time, the flames were already leaping high. Elena had heard Mr. Landon, the science teacher, muttering about the electrical wiring of the old building, saying it was a deathtrap, but Elena knew better. This had to be Damon's work.

Elean jumped as another window shattered, this time under the blast of water from a fire hose. The firemen were putting up a good fight, dragging hoses across the parking lot, working together quickly and efficiently, and had at least contained the fire to only half of the school.

Elena looked around the circle of firelit faces. There was Caroline, her auburn head held high despite the flakes of black ash falling on the parking lot around her. Next to her, Sue Carson huddled under her boyfriend's suit jacket that she had pulled over her thin dress. Vickie Bennett was with a group of jocks and cheerleaders, all quiet and subdued. Even among the kids who hated the school, there were no cheers, no laughter. Everyone was shocked into silence.

An ambulance pulled into the lot, its blue light revolving. One of the paramedics got out and jogged across the lot toward a group of firefighters, calling, "Everybody out?"

The firefighter called back in the affirmative, but Elena's breath caught. She swung around, searching desperately.

"Do you see Stefan anywhere?" she asked the others. They looked around, too, their faces anxious.

*Maybe he was gone before the fire started.*

That didn't make sense, though. Why would Damon start this fire, if Stefan hadn't been here? That was who he wanted to hurt most.

"We'd better tell the fire chief." Matt strode off in the direction of the fire trucks.

*That won't help.*

Fire was one of the few things that could kill a vampire. There wasn't time for the fire fighters to find Stefan. And if they did, it wouldn't be safe, for them or for him.

Elena straightened up, squaring her shoulders. There was no way she was standing uselessly by while Stefan died. Not again.

She had to get past the fire fighters. They were grouped closest to the front of the building, where the fire was at its worst. Over at the side, the school was darker, deserted.

Elena shifted her feet, considering the best way to sneak around the building from where she stood.

"What are you doing?" Bonnie asked.

"I'm going to look for Stefan," Elena told them.

"We'll come with you," Meredith said quickly.

"No," Elena said. "You guys stay here and make sure Stefan isn't outside. If you see him, keep him with you."

"Um, what if we see Damon?" Bonnie asked uneasily. "Do you want us to tell him anything?"

Elena hesitated. Was there any message she could send through her friends that would lessen Damon's anger? She didn't think so. "If you see him, just stay out of his way, okay?" she asked. He was probably long gone, anyway.

She worked her way across the parking lot, sticking to the shadows. As she reached the edge of the lot, she walked between the trees on one side and the cars on the other, eyes on the corner of the school building.

"Get back, miss," a fireman told her as he hurried past. She stepped away from the building, watching him until he had forgotten her and disappeared into the mass of men fighting the flames.

There was a puddle of water at her feet, left by one of the fire hoses. Elena knelt, fumbling at the hem of her dress. She felt a twinge of regret for her beautiful dress as she gripped the crimson silk with both hands and tore. A long strip of silk came off the bottom of the dress. She dipped it into the dirty water of the puddle, soaking the fabric thoroughly.

There was a crash from the far side of the building, something inside collapsing, and, in one motion, the crowd and the fire fighters turned in that direction.

Elena seized her chance and ran, cold water dripping over her hand from the torn piece of her dress. Close up, the fire was *loud*. The flames roared, and the dry wood of the school building snapped and popped as it burned.

Around the corner, it was darker. The flames hadn't reached here yet. A fire exit gaped open, and Elena braced herself and stepped through.

The heat hit her like a wave. A haze of smoke hung in the air, and Elena pressed the wet silk over her nose and mouth to block it out. Her eyes began to water and ache.

Where would Damon have taken Stefan? Nowhere where the fire was burning *yet*, Elena thought. He would want Stefan's suffering more drawn out than that, would want him to hear the crackle of the flames, smell the smoke, and know that the deadly fire—one of the few things that *could* kill Stefan—was getting closer and closer, and that he had no hope of escape. Damon had said he wanted Stefan to suffer.

Of course. She cocked her head to look up the staircase ahead of her. It still looked stable enough. He'd be somewhere high enough that the smoke and heat would rise around him, where he'd feel the flames rising to lick against the floor beneath him. Damon would have put Stefan in the bell tower.

Elena climbed. The silk at her mouth filtered out the worst of the smoke, but she still choked and gasped, each breath coming with more difficulty than the last. Heavy boots clumped through the halls on the other side of the building. Fire fighters, she supposed, but she saw no one, just the heavy haze of smoke.

From somewhere below came the crash of a falling support beam, and the floor underfoot shook. Elena grabbed at the banister to steady herself, then sped up. She wobbled, and her feet ached as she ran. High heels were no good for this, but bare feet would be worse, so she had to keep going.

On the third floor, the staircase ended. She peered around, trying to spot the entrance to the bell tower through the worsening smoke. Her eyes burned, and she coughed—the wet silk was drying, it wasn't protecting her enough now.

There it was. She crossed the hall and laid her hand against the wood of the small door to the bell tower. It was cool still, no fire behind it. But the knob wouldn't turn.

It was locked; of course it was locked. The school didn't want the students messing around up here. Elena squeezed her eyes shut against the smoke. What was she going to do?

She tugged at the door again, and then began to throw herself against it. She had to get through. "Stefan!" she called. "Stefan! Can you hear me?"

There was no answer.

The door wasn't made to withstand a continuous assault. Elena threw all her weight against it over and over, ignoring the bruises she could feel blossoming on her shoulder and side. At last, the flimsy lock broke, and the door burst open. She tumbled through and fell to her knees, gasping and coughing.

Elena scrambled back to her feet and up the narrow rickety staircase to the top of the tower. Beneath the heavy bronze bell, archways opened on all four sides, and at last she could breathe. She staggered to one of the arches and took a few deep breaths, looking out over the parking lot below. Police cars were pulling in now, their red and blue lights flashing.

Her head was spinning less now that she had taken a few gulps of air, and Elena turned back around to look at the inside of the bell tower.

There was a weak motion, down in the darkest corner of the cupola. A small sound, barely more than a whimper. Elena crossed toward it and fell to her knees. There was a huddled dark shape there, and he shifted to stare up at her. Stefan mumbled something, his voice thick and choked.

"It's all right," she said automatically, running her fingers soothingly through his hair. He was tied up, and there was a band of fabric across his mouth, pulled viciously tight.

He flinched under her hand, scrabbling back toward the wall. He didn't seem to recognize her. She worked her hands beneath the gag, trying to untie its tight knot with her fingers. She couldn't loosen it.

She fumbled around on the floor, feeling around in the dark for something sharp. The floor was hot beneath her hands and knees—the fire must be rising below them.

Her fingers closed around a sharp-edged stone, and she worked it against the gag, feeling the cloth's fibers rip. Finally, it came loose and she pulled it away from Stefan's mouth.

As she removed the gag, something else spilled over his lips. Elena leaned closer, bracing herself with one hand on the rough brickwork above Stefan's head, squinting to see what was there.

Thin stalks of vervain sputtered out of Stefan's mouth. He gagged and choked as he spit them out. Anger rushed through Elena, as hot and sudden as a bolt of lightning.

"How dare he?" she muttered. "How *dare* he?" Damon had stuffed his brother's mouth with vervain, muting his powers and muddling his mind. And then he had left him to die, alone, confused, and in pain.

Heedless of Stefan's sharp canines this time, she used two fingers to scoop out more of the vervain clogging his mouth. One tooth scraped her finger stingingly, but she barely noticed.

As his mouth emptied, she could hear Stefan breathing, long, ragged hoarse breaths. She pushed her forefinger in again, checking that she had gotten every piece.

Stefan's tongue dragged slowly against her finger. Elena hesitated, and he latched on, sucking desperately at the cut on her finger.

After a moment, Stefan's eyelashes fluttered and his eyes slowly opened. He stared at Elena for a second before recognition filtered into his gaze. Abruptly, he pulled away.

"Elena," he said roughly, and panic flashed across his pale face. "I ... don't know how to explain this."

The bricks beneath Elena's knees were getting uncomfortably hot now. The fire must be climbing. "We have to get out of here," she said, her pulse pounding.

Stefan's eyes widened, and he strained visibly. The ropes around his wrists snapped first, and then the ones around his ankles. Without the vervain, they couldn't hold him. He began, slowly, to climb to his feet. "Is the door blocked?" he asked.

"I-I think so," Elena said. "The fire was spreading really fast."

Stefan shook his head as if he was shaking off the last of the vervain's effects. "Trust me," he said. Drawing Elena up into his arms, Stefan climbed into the archway.

Holding her tightly, Stefan leaped into the night.

## 18

"Who *are* you?" Stefan asked. "How did you find me tonight?" After their leap from the school, he'd brought her back to his room at Mrs. Flowers' boarding house. He leaned against the wall by the window, his finely drawn features so pale they could have been carved out of marble.

Elena clasped her hands in her lap. "I knew that Damon must have started the fire, and, after what he said to you, I had a feeling that he wouldn't have let you make it out," she said slowly.

Stefan pinched the bridge of his nose between two fingers, as if his head hurt. "And how do you know Damon?"

"I met him in the graveyard." It seemed wise to stick to the simplest answer.

Coming a step closer, Stefan narrowed his eyes. "You knew what was going on with the vervain. It didn't surprise you or scare you when we leaped from the bell tower, or when I fed from you. You know what Damon and I are."

There was something threatening about Stefan now as he almost loomed above her. Elena raised her hands in surrender, doing her best to look harmless. "I'm not your enemy," she said. "Yours or Damon's. I only want to help."

She hoped that her sincerity shone through. All she wanted to do was to save them both.

Stefan leaned back against the wall. Rubbing a hand across his face, he laughed, a miserable, rough laugh. "There's nothing *to* help, Elena. Damon and I are monsters, and the sooner we get out of this town the better off everyone else will be. If I leave here, he'll follow me. You'll be safe." Shaking his head, he added, "I should have known better than to try, to pretend to be human."

"No, Stefan, please," Elena was out of her chair without even thinking about it. Reaching out to take Stefan's hands in her own, she squeezed them tightly. "It wasn't a mistake." He shook his head and started to pull away, and Elena stepped closer still, looking up into his eyes. "We can work together. We can keep Damon under control. You don't have to be alone."

Stefan eyes grew darker as he held Elena's gaze. And then he bent his head to her lips. For a moment, it was as if the whole world was just the two of them, heat rushing through Elena's body.

It was all so familiar. They were both filthy and stinking of smoke, but it could have been the night of their first Homecoming—when Stefan had rescued her from Tyler in the graveyard and brought her here. Maybe it was destiny after all. They were always going to end up here, tired and drained, secrets stretching the space between them.

At the thought, Elena pulled away, suddenly cold as she stepped out of Stefan's arms.

"I'm sorry," Elena stammered. "I didn't mean … I can't do this right now." She felt as if the world was shifting under her feet.

Stefan turned away so she couldn't quite see his face. "I apologize," he said. "I'll take you home."

Elena followed him down the darkened stairway, brushing her fingers against her lips. *This is all my fault*, she thought, as she left the boardinghouse and crossed the dirt driveway to Stefan's low, black Porsche. If she hadn't kissed Stefan, if Damon hadn't seen her, things between them wouldn't be deteriorating. The school wouldn't have burned down today.

Stefan's car was just as smooth and luxurious a ride as Damon's. The engine's purr was the only sound in the car as Elena and Stefan sat silently, each wrapped in their own thoughts. Stefan's eyes were fixed on the road, and his body was stiff with tension. Elena sighed and wrapped her arms around herself.

How could Stefan and Damon hate each other so much? Elena thought of the rueful affection she'd seen grow between the brothers over the past few years in her own life. They played pool together. They fenced and played cards, all the entertainments they'd both learned to pass the time over the centuries. They fought side by side, graceful and deadly.

The brothers always came back together when it mattered most. They'd saved each other's lives more than once.

Elena remembered Damon's fury after Stefan's death. And more, she remembered the pure despair on his face, the way he had looked as he told her that now there was no one, no one at all, who remembered him when he was alive, when he was a human. He'd lost his past.

How had they gotten from *here* to *there*?

Then, as Stefan's car purred around the corner onto Elena's street, she finally got it. The loneliness in Stefan's eyes, his room carefully designed for one monastic, solitary life. Damon's vicious hatred for his little brother, paired with the fact that, wherever Stefan went, Damon watched him from afar. Even in tonight's fire, Damon had left him far away from the flames. If Stefan hadn't gotten away, would Damon have come back for him?

They always came back to each other.

Stefan and Damon were each other's *family*, all they had left. And all their love and history might have gotten tangled up into one big ball of resentment and anger, but that didn't mean it wasn't still there. She knew it was still there. She'd seen it in the future, as strong as ever.

Maybe it wasn't Elena who had changed Damon, back in her own time. Mylea had said that love would save Damon, would save them all. But it wasn't Elena's love that would do it.

From now on, she realized with a blinding flash, she wasn't going to try to make Damon fall in love with her.

Instead, she needed to fix Stefan and Damon. If they could just be *brothers* again, everything else would fall into place.

Stefan pulled up in front of Elena's house and stopped. Her front door flew open, and Aunt Judith and Robert rushed out onto the lawn. No doubt they'd heard about the fire.

Before she opened the car door to reassure them, Elena turned to Stefan and laid her hand over his.

"I know what we have to do now. We can fix everything," she told him, feeling strong and sure. "Tomorrow, we're going to look for Damon."

*ear Diary,*

*I woke up this morning and I
wished I were dead.*

*Not really, I suppose. If I meant it, I would just
let things take their course. Grab at the chance of a
brief happiness with Stefan, knowing that it will
lead to so much suffering, to the destruction of all
three of us.*

*But Damon was so full of anger. The way he
looked at me when he found me in Stefan's arms—he
never looked at me that way before, even when things
between us were at their worst. Like he* hated *me.*

Elena glanced at the clock. She needed to leave for
school soon. Downstairs, she could hear the familiar clatter

of Aunt Judith making breakfast. It felt so much like the morning when Damon had driven her to school, when it had seemed like everything was falling into place. She began to write again.

*I refuse to believe that I've ruined everything.*

*If I can just show Damon how much Stefan still loves him, how much they need each other, maybe things will turn out okay after all. I have to believe that. I can't give up on us, not yet.*

* * *

"One day off," Bonnie fumed, flicking her red curls over her shoulder as the two girls crossed the parking lot together. "We go through a completely traumatizing event, and they can't give us even one day off."

"It's amazing how quickly they pulled all this together, though," Elena commented. In daylight, she could see that the school hadn't *entirely* burned down.

One side of the building, where the office and most of the classrooms were, was charred and half-collapsed. Elena couldn't suppress a shudder as she looked at the bell tower. The staircase she had climbed to find Stefan must be entirely gone. But the other side, where the auditorium and cafeteria were, looked mostly solid even though stained a dirty gray by the smoke. The heavy smell of ash hung over everything.

Behind the school now stood a row of temporary white trailers to be used as classrooms for the rest of the year, until the school could be rebuilt. All around the trailers, students gathered in groups, leaning eagerly toward each other to gossip. Harried administrators were trying to shepherd everyone into the right trailers. Everything seemed to be in only slightly controlled chaos.

"See you later," Bonnie called as she veered off into chemistry, and Elena found the trailer where her trig class was. Meredith was already there, her homework laid out neatly in front of her.

As Elena settled into the desk beside her, Meredith looked up with a worried frown. "Have you heard the gossip?" she asked. "Everyone's saying that Stefan started the fire."

Elena remembered with a twinge of dismay the low, excited, I've-got-a-secret tone to the whispers before class.

They'd been here before. It might start at the high school, but the rumors would spread all over town. Adults would get upset. Stefan would be shunned.

"That's ridiculous," she said sharply.

Meredith bit her lip. "There's no real evidence. Everyone used to think the way he keeps to himself was romantic, but now they're saying it's creepy. He disappeared from the dance right before the fire started."

"So did *we*," Elena objected.

"*We* were all together." Meredith dipped her head, shuffling the papers around on her desk. "I don't want to believe it, but it is strange how Stefan disappeared. When Matt told the fire fighters that Stefan wasn't there, they started searching for him to make sure he wasn't in the building. You said you didn't see him when you looked either."

Elena winced. It had seemed simpler when she got home just to call Bonnie and Meredith and tell them she had given up and decided to leave. Now it was too late to pretend to have run into Stefan.

"They found him back at his boardinghouse. When the police questioned him he was *covered* in smoke and ash." Meredith raised her head, her gray eyes troubled. "I'm not saying Stefan did anything. And I promise not to tell anyone that Damon was there, either. But maybe you should stay away from both of them, Elena."

"Anybody could have set that fire!" Elena said, her voice a little too loud. The teacher looked up from her desk inquiringly, and Elena lowered her voice. "It was probably somebody sneaking a cigarette."

Meredith's forehead creased in concern. "Elena, you don't even know Stefan. You've been avoiding him since he started school. And then, suddenly, you've kissed him—*once*—and now you won't hear anything against him? I thought you were with Damon."

"I am, but—" Elena began.

"Okay, time to stop the chatter and review your home-work assignments," Ms. Halpern said, stepping up to the front of the room. With one more worried glance, Meredith turned away from Elena to face the teacher.

Elena chewed on her lip. This was worse than the first time she had been here. Then, everyone had started sus-pecting Stefan of being responsible for Mr. Tanner's mur-der after Halloween. The gossip had spread until, despite the lack of any real evidence, everyone was convinced Stefan was the killer. Aunt Judith had banned Elena from seeing Stefan, and some of the adults in town—Tyler's dad, especially—had been ready to form a lynch mob and attack him.

Now, because of Elena, all the suspicion and hatred for Stefan was starting earlier. And, that time, at least Meredith and Bonnie had been on her side. They hadn't had any more proof of Stefan's innocence then than they did now, but they had believed Elena when she swore he was innocent. They'd believed her because they knew she knew Stefan.

Elena wrapped her arms around herself, suddenly cold. If Fell's Church turned against Stefan earlier, maybe it would all happen earlier. Was Elena doomed to drive off Wickery Bridge and drown, no matter what she did? She could almost feel that icy dark water rising around her.

Was it hopeless for her to try to fight fate? Was Stefan doomed to die? Would Elena end up back in that cold gray in-between place, heading for death?

The rest of the morning, Elena kept an eye out for Stefan whenever she moved from one trailer classroom to another, but she never saw him. Crowds of students gathered on the crumbling black asphalt between the trailers, talking in low, excited voices. Elena hoped Stefan had come to school today. Nothing would fan the flames of the rumor more than if it seemed that Stefan was hiding.

When she got to history class, Stefan's seat was empty. Elena's shoulders slumped. Mr. Tanner began to lecture about the English Civil War, and Elena stared down at her notebook, her eyes stinging.

"I see you've decided to grace us with your presence, Mr. Salvatore." Mr. Tanner's voice was whip-sharp. Elena lifted her head.

Stefan, grim-faced, hesitated in the doorway. Mr. Tanner waved an arm in an exaggerated gesture of courtesy. "Please, take a seat," he said. "We're all so glad you decided to wander in."

Stefan sat down without glancing at Elena. He bent his head over his desk. His shoulders were stiffly set, betraying his awareness of the gossip and hatred buzzing around him. Elena sighed. He probably thought it was deserved, even though he hadn't started the fire. Stefan, the Stefan of now, thought he was a monster and that people *should* fear and hate him.

Elena sat up straight and glared around the classroom. The girls beside Stefan, who had been nudging each other and whispering, exchanged a glance and turned back to their books with new interest.

Caroline, though, stared straight back at Elena, her lips turning up in a smirk. Tilting her head, she whispered something to the girl next to her, her eyes never leaving Elena's, and her smile widened. She and the other girl both laughed.

At least Dick and Tyler's desks were empty, since they were still suspended. It was Tyler who had whipped up a frenzy against Stefan last time. Tyler was a bully, he always had been. Elena sighed and pressed a hand against her forehead.

Was everything bound to slide toward the same ends, no matter what she did? Were some things inevitable?

No. She couldn't believe that. She pulled back her shoulders and sat up straight, running a cold eye over Caroline, who was still smirking. When the other girl finally looked away, Elena felt a jolt of satisfaction. Elena was still the queen of the school after all.

When class finally ended, Elena shot out of her seat and grabbed Stefan's arm, pulling him aside before he could leave the trailer classroom.

"You're not afraid to be seen with me?" he asked softly, his head down, eyes fixed on the ugly gray carpeting of the trailer. "They're right not to trust me, Elena."

"Don't be ridiculous," she told him, meeting the hostile looks of the other students as they edged past. Bonnie hesitated in the doorway, eyeing Stefan, and Elena gave her a quick, reassuring smile.

"Call me later," Bonnie said pleadingly as she left.

Once the trailer was empty, Elena turned back to Stefan. She was still gripping his jacketed arm, so tightly that her fingers ached, but he barely seemed to notice. "We don't have much time," she told him. "We need a game plan. We need to get Damon under control."

Stefan huffed a short, bitter laugh. "Damon's never under control."

"Stefan, look at me." Letting go of his sleeve, Elena reached up and framed Stefan's face with her hands. His skin was cool, and his cheekbones were strong and wide beneath her fingers. She waited for him to bring his eyes up to meet hers, her heart beating hard as the connection between them slid into place, that sense of recognition and almost magnetic attraction. His face cradled in her hands, Stefan blinked as if he was seeing her for the first time.

"Don't give up," she said, trying to put the weight of all the secret knowledge she had—all the things she couldn't tell him in words—behind what she said. "You're the only one who can change things with your brother. I believe in you."

Stefan gently pulled away from her hands, and Elena ached as their contact broke. His face was sorrowful. "I don't think that Damon can change," he said. "But I think I know where he is."

## 20

Unlike the neatly maintained, modern part of the graveyard where Elena's parents lay, the section dating back to the Civil War was overgrown and crumbling. Long creepers draped themselves across worn gray tombstones, and the ground was uneven beneath Elena's feet. Half-broken weeping saints and angels loomed overhead, and the dark, iron-barred fronts of the mausoleums gave Elena the sense that anyone could be watching them.

"I don't understand why you think Damon would be *here*," she said, stumbling over a broken tombstone hidden in the grass. She grabbed Stefan's arm to keep from falling.

"This is exactly the place Damon would be," Stefan said, his gaze moving watchfully from the ruined church to a mausoleum half concealed by overgrown yew trees. "He thinks acting like a creature of the night is funny. He wants death all around him."

Elena frowned. It didn't really sound like Damon to *her*. The Damon she knew liked clean, modern lines. And he loved luxury. He didn't stay anywhere long, but the houses and apartments she'd seen Damon live in were rich and elegant. He filled them with every possible comfort but almost nothing personal, nothing he wouldn't be willing to leave behind. He didn't court the trimmings of death.

Stefan glanced down at her with a slight, bitter smile. "How well do you know my brother really, Elena? You see what he wants you to see."

Elena shook her head, but didn't answer. Stefan had a point. If she really had met Damon just a few weeks ago, how well could she have known him?

Elena's eyes lingered on the ruined church. It was half-collapsed, most of the roof fallen in. Only three of its walls were standing.

Katherine was underneath there, in the old church's crypt. She might be watching them at this very moment. There was no trace of fog, no cold wind, no blue-eyed white kitten prowling in the dead grass around the church. If Katherine was there, she was lying low, content to watch for now.

When Stefan turned toward the church, Elena nudged him away. "Let's look in the mausoleums," she said.

The grim mausoleums made of granite and iron scattered around the old churchyard. Each housed the bones of a family of original settlers of Fell's Church. They were dark and forbidding now, overgrown with ivy, their flagstone paths pitted by time. One had the Gilbert name, Elena's father's family, but she didn't know much about the people whose bones laid there, except that one had been a young soldier killed in the Civil War.

Elena and Stefan slipped into an easy routine, working their way clockwise from one mausoleum to the next around the churchyard. Elena would stand lookout while Stefan forced each narrow door.

There was no sign of Damon in the Gilbert mausoleum, only three gray stone coffins and a dusty vase, which must have once been used for flowers. The space inside was claustrophobically narrow, its air stale, and Elena was glad to back out again after one quick look.

Surely if Damon were living here, he would have chosen her family's mausoleum, as some sort of elaborate tease. Elena stumbled as they moved on to the next small tomb, and Stefan steadied her. "Careful," he said. "The ground's uneven."

Elena cast a glance across to the newer part of the graveyard. "I'm more worried about someone catching us vandalizing graves than I am about tripping," she said.

Stefan cocked his head, sending Power out around the graveyard. "There's no one here," he said. He looked drawn and tired. He probably hadn't fed recently enough to be able to Influence anyone into forgetting about them if they were caught breaking into the tombs.

Elena stood by the next mausoleum and looked up at the ruins of the church as she listened to the grating noise of Stefan forcing the tomb's door. At least she had the rest of the vervain in her pocket. If Katherine came out of the catacombs, she wouldn't be able to Influence Elena.

"There," Stefan said with satisfaction. Elena stopped staring at the church and jostled her way in beside him.

It was as gray and dusty as the others had been, but the tops of the two tombs inside had been swept clean. On one sat a pile of neatly folded dark clothing. Elena rifled through it: all black, all designer, all clearly expensive. Some of them she had seen Damon wearing. The other tomb held a folded blanket and a thin leather bound book.

Elena picked up the book. It was in Italian, and seemed to be a book of verse. "Stefan, what—" she began. A loud groan of rusted metal interrupted her, and, before she could move, the door to the tomb slammed shut. A huge thud followed, something terribly heavy slamming into the outside of the mausoleum. The small building shook, and Elena screamed, a high, thin noise.

Then there was silence. With the door closed, it was pitch-black inside the tomb. For a moment, Elena could hear nothing but the pounding of her own heart. From the other side of the tomb, Stefan swore.

"Stefan?" Elena asked, her voice rising.

Starting toward Stefan and the tomb's door, she banged her elbow hard against something in the dark. "Ouch," she said, and rubbed at it, tears prickling at the back of her eyes.

"Keep still," Stefan said. She didn't even hear him coming toward her, but suddenly he was touching her gently, running his hands over her arm.

"I don't think anything's broken," he told her. "You'll have a bruise, though."

"Are we stuck in here?" Elena's voice wavered, despite herself. She was suddenly, terrifyingly aware of the dead all around her. The tomb she stood beside was full of moldering bones.

There was a short pause, and then Stefan spoke, sounding grimmer than before. "Damon's shut us in. I tried the door, but I can't force it. There must be something jammed up against it, holding it closed."

"Oh." For the first time, Elena noticed how cold it was inside the mausoleum, the cold of a stone place that never felt the sun. She shivered.

"We'll find a way out of here," Stefan said, his voice lightening. "Or someone will come." Suddenly, his hands were around her waist and he lifted her gently. In a second, she was sitting on the cold top of the tomb, and Stefan was beside her, wrapping his jacket around her shoulders.

For a while, they sat in silence. Stefan was reassuringly solid beside her and, after a while, Elena let herself lean slightly against him.

Who would come for them? It was rare that someone came into this part of the cemetery, even rarer after dark, and night was coming. Elena felt a clutch of panic in her chest, and her breath got shorter. She didn't want to stay here.

"Stefan," she said. She turned her head toward his.

"What is it, Elena?"

"There is a way for you to get us out of here." She brushed her hair away from her neck, dipping her head in a clear invitation.

Stefan's breath caught and he shifted away, his slight warmth disappearing from her side. When he spoke again, he sounded choked. "I can't."

"You can. If you're going to save us, you need the strength my blood will give you."

"Elena." Stefan sounded panicked, and she automatically reached for his hand in the dark to reassure him. "I haven't fed from a human being for a long time. I tried once, not long ago"—*The man under the bridge*, Elena's mind supplied—"and I couldn't control myself. I don't want to hurt you."

"You won't," Elena told him, hanging onto his cold hand. "I trust you." He still hesitated, and she added, "It's the only way out of here, Stefan."

With a small, soft sigh of surrender, Stefan bent his head to her throat.

It had been so *long* since she had been with Stefan like this. Elena's eyes filled with tears of joy and sorrow at the familiar twin pricks of pain as his canines slid beneath her skin. His lips were gentle against her throat, and his pulse was speeding to pound in time with hers.

Elena tried to hold back the memories that were tumbling through her mind: the night she had pledged to be Stefan's forever—*sleek and elegant in his best suit, his eyes wide and wondering, greener than ever*—the first night they had kissed, after Homecoming in that other world—*the look of helpless desire as he bent his head to hers*—the incredulity and horror in his face when she was reborn as a vampire and at first forgot who they were to each other—*the pure defeat on his face as he let her claw at him.* The life they'd built together. The warmth and comfort she'd found in his arms as he'd held Elena close.

Even though she kept the memories from him, Elena couldn't help some of her emotions pouring through the careful wall they'd constructed between them. Love and tenderness and regret. Pain and joy. Guilt. Passion.

It was enough that, as he slowly withdrew his canines from her throat, Stefan cupped her face for a moment, his fingers cool against her skin. She could see nothing through the darkness, but Elena thought he was staring into her eyes. "Who *are* you?" he whispered, just as he had the night of the fire.

"Someone who cares about you," Elena whispered. *Please,* she thought desperately, *please let me save him.*

Stefan's hand lingered on Elena's face for a moment, just a gentle brush of skin on skin, and then he was gone.

Over at the door, Elena heard a great, creaking crash, and then light appeared, flooding through the crack as Stefan forced the door open. There was a rustling, the sound of breaking branches, and finally a huge thud.

"You can come out now," Stefan said, a dark shape against the light of the doorway.

Elena came through, squinting. It was brisk outside, although not with the heavy bone-chilling cold of the tomb, and the sun was setting. It was almost dark, really; it just seemed bright after the pitch blackness.

A huge oak tree lay across the churchyard, its branches brushing the door of the mausoleum where they had been trapped. It had been ripped out of the ground; Elena could see the great pit in the earth left by its roots.

"It was jammed up against the door," Stefan told her.

Now that Elena's eyes had adjusted to the evening light, she noticed the long, already healing scrapes on his arms from the tree's branches. Stefan gazed past her, and Elena turned, following his eyes to the dent in the mausoleum's stone façade, where the tree had slammed against it.

There was so much rage in the way the tree had been torn out of the earth and thrown against the stone tomb. Elena's stomach twisted nervously. She might love Damon, but he had no love left for them.

## 21

It was fully dark by the time Elena slipped through her front door. She could feel her whole body relax at being home at last. The tall Victorian house where she'd lived since she was born felt clean and bright and warm, its heavy curtains shutting out the darkness. From the kitchen, she could hear the clatter of pans and smell a chicken roasting.

"Dinner in twenty minutes," Aunt Judith called cheerfully. Elena called back an acknowledgement, staring at herself in the mirror by the door. She looked tired and disheveled, her hair matted and a streak of dirt across her forehead. There was a purpling bruise on her throat where Stefan had bitten her, twin dots of dried blood in its center, and she pulled her shirt collar up to cover it.

"You're home!" Margaret thudded down the stairs and leaped toward Elena, catching her around the waist in a bear hug. "I missed you."

"I missed you, too," Elena said, laughing. "All day long." She bent to press her cheek against her little sister's soft hair and breathed in the Play-Doh and baby shampoo scent of her.

Pulling away, Margaret grinned up at her. "Your friend came over looking for you," she said. "He gave me this." She pulled a lollipop out of her pocket and waved it in triumph.

Elena examined the candy. It was a pink rose made out of thin slivers of almost-translucent hard candy. "Pretty," she said. "Matt gave you this?" Matt had a soft spot for Margaret, and he was always bringing her little treats.

"No, your friend Damon gave it to me," Margaret said, and tried to take the lollipop back.

A wave of panic washed over Elena, and her fingers tightened automatically on the candy. Elena had invited him into her home. How could she have been so stupid?

"Give it," Margaret said, pulling on the candy.

"No, wait," Elena said, but Margaret yanked the lollipop out of her hand, pulled it out of the wrapper, and defiantly stuck it into her mouth before Elena could snatch it back.

*It was wrapped*, Elena reassured herself as she watched her baby sister eat the candy with evident enjoyment.

Poison wasn't really Damon's style. If he had wanted to hurt Margaret or Aunt Judith, he would have done it more directly. No, this had just been a warning. Damon was letting Elena know that he could get to her family whenever he wanted.

"Listen to me, Margaret," she said, squatting so that she was eye to eye with her little sister. "Damon's not my friend, okay? If he comes here again, stay away from him."

Margaret frowned. "He was really nice," she said. "I don't know why you don't want to be friends with him."

Was it Margaret saying this, or was it something Damon had told her to say, Elena wondered. What if Damon had used his Power to Influence her little sister? She looked into Margaret's sky-blue eyes, trying to see if there was anything off about her, any sign that her words were not her own.

The Damon that Elena loved wouldn't have used his Power on a child, Elena thought. He would have considered it ungentlemanly and beneath him. With a heavy, sick feeling, she admitted to herself that she didn't know exactly what the Damon of this time was capable of.

"Meggie, can you come put the napkins on the table for me, please?" Aunt Judith called from the kitchen, and Margaret twisted out of Elena's hands and was gone without a word.

Elena headed up the stairs, her steps slow and heavy. She had to think. There must be some way to get Aunt Judith and Margaret away from here. She couldn't let them get hurt, and she couldn't let Damon use them as pawns to hurt Elena.

By the time she reached the top of the stairs, Elena had made up her mind. She went into the bathroom and grabbed a towel. Pulling off one of her shoes, she wrapped the towel around it and then opened the hall window. Outside, the branches of the quince tree almost brushed the window frame. It was close enough that someone could conceivably climb inside, although it would be a dangerous stretch.

Bracing herself, she slammed the heel of the shoe against the window's catch. The towel muffled the sound of the blow, but not as much as Elena had hoped. She paused and listened. Aunt Judith was running water downstairs, and under the noise of the water, Elena could hear both the television and Margaret singing to herself. Trusting in the noise downstairs to cover the thuds, Elena slammed the heel of her shoe against the window catch again and again until it finally bent and twisted, breaking.

With a sharp crack, the pane of glass below the catch shattered, broken glass falling in shards onto the hall carpet. Elena froze. She hadn't expected that. Still, maybe it made the whole scene more convincing.

Quickly and quietly, Elena picked up a silver candle-stick from the windowsill. She took a carved jade box from a little table in the hall and a small marble figure of an angel that her parents had once brought home from Italy from another. Hurrying into her room, she slipped her shoe back on, wrapped the objects in the towel, and shoved the bundled towel deep into her closet.

After one last glance around to make sure everything was concealed, she went back to stand in front of the broken hall window, took a deep breath, and screamed.

There was a sudden, shocked silence downstairs, followed by a flurry of movement. "Elena?" Aunt Judith called worriedly, running up the stairs. "What happened? Are you all right?"

Elena turned to meet her as she reached the top of the stairs. "I think someone broke in," she said. She was so full of dread that it was easy to infuse the words with fear.

As Elena pointed them out, Aunt Judith examined the broken catch, the smashed windowpane, and the spots where knickknacks were missing from the hall. Looking in her own room and Elena's, she saw that nothing else seemed to be missing.

"I don't know," she said finally, doubtfully. "A branch could have blown against the window and broken it. It seems strange to me that a thief would take just three little objects, and nothing else. All my jewelry's still here, and I had some money on my dresser that's completely untouched."

Elena wanted to scream with frustration. She didn't have to try hard at all to bring tears to her eyes or a waver to her voice.

"Please, Aunt Judith," she said. "I really don't think any of us should sleep here tonight. Can't you and Margaret go to Robert's, at least until we can get someone to fix the window? Anyone could come in."

Aunt Judith hesitated. "What about you, Elena?" she asked. "I'm certainly not going to leave you here all alone."

"I can go to Meredith's," Elena said quickly. "It's closer to school, and her parents won't mind."

Convincing Aunt Judith was agonizing. A hundred times, she wondered if they were just being hysterical and almost changed her mind about leaving the house. Once she *had* finally agreed to leave the house, she insisted on them all sitting down and eating dinner together.

Elena could barely nibble the juicy roast chicken even though she recognized that it was delicious. Her eyes kept straying to the darkness beyond the dining room windows. Was Damon out there? She could imagine him in his crow form, huddled on a branch and watching her with bright, malicious eyes.

By the time Robert's gray Volvo turned into the drive, Elena felt like she was almost bursting out of her skin with anxious, restless energy. They had to *go*. They had to get away, before it was too late.

Grabbing her sister with one hand and both their bags with the other, Elena hustled Margaret out to the car, ignoring her protests, and buckled her securely into her booster seat.

"Do you want me to check the window?" Robert said, politely getting out of the car to take Aunt Judith's bag and open the passenger's side door for her.

"No!" said Elena sharply before Aunt Judith could answer. When they both looked at her in surprise, she gave them a small, weak smile. "Sorry. I'm just so nervous. Can't we get out of here?"

As they pulled out of the driveway, Elena settled watchfully in the backseat next to Margaret, her overnight bag clutched in her lap. She felt sure that nothing would happen to them on the drive over to Meredith's. And then, after they dropped her off, she could only hope that Damon would lose interest in them. At least he'd never been invited into Robert's house. Getting Aunt Judith and Margaret as far away from her as she could seemed like the only way to protect them.

\* \* \*

"This is the best part," Bonnie said as she rolled onto her stomach on Meredith's bed, her eyes fixed on the TV screen a few feet away. "After he kisses her, you know they're going to get past all the stuff that came between them."

"I still think she should have ended up with her friend instead," Meredith said critically from where she leaned against the headboard. "That was the first ending, you know, and the test audiences hated it so much that they reshot it."

"And rightly so," Bonnie said. "Bleah."

Elena laughed and jostled against her. "There's nothing wrong with him. I think he's cute."

"Bleah," Bonnie said again, wrinkling her nose.

The sick, dread-filled feeling in the pit of Elena's stomach hadn't gone away for a moment. But, despite all of that, it was good to be here once more. When Bonnie had heard that Elena was spending the night, she had invited herself over, too. The warm smell of baking cookies rose comfortingly from the kitchen downstairs.

"Hey, would you braid my hair?" Bonnie asked, as the couple on screen finally kissed.

"Sure," Elena said, and Bonnie wiggled around so that her back was to Elena.

"Do you want a French braid?" Elena asked. Bonnie nodded, and Elena began separating the curling strands of Bonnie's hair just as the oven timer went off downstairs.

"I've got it," Meredith said, hopping up.

"Wait, I'll come with you," Elena told her, letting go of Bonnie's curls.

"I think I can handle it," Meredith said wryly.

After a moment of hesitation, Elena took hold of Bonnie's hair again. This was Meredith's house, and Damon wasn't invited in. She would be fine.

"So ..." Bonnie said playfully as Meredith left the room. "Who's the better kisser, Stefan or Damon?"

Elena winced. "It's not that easy."

"Easy or not, I bet they're both pretty good, aren't they?" Bonnie asked. Elena could hear the cheeky grin in her voice.

Heat flooded Elena's cheeks. She thought of the nostalgic emotions that had washed through her as Stefan kissed and, darker and more intimate, the way it had felt when Damon had drunk her blood. "Yeah," she admitted in a tiny voice.

"Uh-huh," Bonnie said smugly. Then she twisted around to look at Elena, her brown eyes bright with sincerity. "If you say Stefan didn't set the fire, I believe you, Elena."

"I know he didn't," Elena said.

"*Mmm.* He's much too cute to be a psycho."

Elena laughed despite herself. "I'm not sure that's the best way to tell."

She busied herself twining Bonnie's hair into an elegant braid. "There," she said, after a few minutes. "Gorgeous."

Bonnie bounced to her feet. Going to the full-length mirror hanging on the back of Meredith's closet door, she turned her head from side to side, admiring herself. "Nice. Thank you."

As she watched Bonnie, Elena became aware of a niggling sense of something not quite right.

"Does it seem to you like Meredith's taking a really long time?" she asked.

Eyes still on her own reflection, Bonnie lifted one shoulder in a shrug. "I know, right?" she said. "How long does it take to put some cookies on a plate? I'm starving."

"That's not what I mean," Elena began, and then the door opened and her shoulders sagged with relief. Meredith was back.

"About time," Bonnie said cheerfully, and grabbed a cookie.

"Careful, they're hot," Meredith said, smiling. Then she caught Elena's eye and her smile faded. "What's wrong?"

Elena felt like she was frozen in place. Looped around Meredith's neck was a deep red scarf that she certainly hadn't been wearing when she went downstairs.

"Why are you wearing that?" she said, her voice cracking. "Take it off."

Bonnie and Meredith looked at each other, their eyebrows lifting. "Um … Elena?" Bonnie asked. "What are you talking about?"

"The scarf!" Elena insisted. "Take it off right now!" She should have gone downstairs with Meredith. It had been stupid of her to think they would be safe, just because Damon hadn't yet been invited into Meredith's house. Even if he hadn't had his Power, Damon would have been able to charm and talk his way into almost anywhere. *With* all the Power at his command, all he would have to do was ask. And Meredith was defenseless: She didn't even know that Damon was someone to be afraid of.

"I don't know what your problem is, Elena," Meredith grumbled, slowly unwrapping the scarf from around her throat. "I was cold, okay? It's freezing downstairs. And I think this looks nice."

Elena stared. Unwilling to trust her eyes, she went closer and, ignoring Meredith's startled objections, brushed the other girl's hair aside and inspected her neck. It was smooth and unmarked. No vampire had touched her.

"Hey!" Meredith finally said, stepping back and staring at Elena. "Personal space! Please."

"Sorry, sorry. I thought there was something on your throat." Elena felt ridiculous.

"Like a mole or something?" Meredith said uneasily, rubbing the side of her neck.

"I don't know. Like a shadow, I guess."

Elena felt sick. Damon could get to them easily here if he wanted to. Was she putting Bonnie and Meredith in danger by staying here?

The other girls picked up on Elena's change in mood, and after only a little while, Bonnie stretched and said, with forced brightness, "Well, I'm wiped out."

"We should get to bed," Meredith agreed. "I've got a French test tomorrow."

Bonnie shared Meredith's double bed, and the loveseat in the corner of the bedroom unfolded into a narrow single bed for Elena. After they had all climbed into bed and Meredith had switched out the light, Elena thought of something.

"Hey," she called softly across the divide between their beds. "Do you still have the vervain I gave you?"

"The *what?*" Bonnie asked sleepily.

"The vervain. The plants I gave you after Homecoming. Do you still have them?"

"The weeds?" Bonnie's voice was puzzled. "I don't know what happened to them. They probably fell out of my hair. There was a fire going on, remember?"

"Meredith?"

"No," Meredith said, sounding exasperated. She sat up and turned on the light. "I don't remember what happened to the dried-out weeds you gave me at Homecoming."

For a moment, Elena thought of telling them everything. They were her friends. And they were smart and brave; they'd been her allies through thick and thin. If they knew what was going on, they could help her. And they would be better able to protect themselves.

She licked her suddenly dry lips and took a quick breath. But it was that knowledge that had ruined their lives. She couldn't do that to them, not again.

"I ... I'm sorry, you guys," she said. "I know I'm acting weird. Just promise me you'll be careful." She would have to get more vervain and give it to them, hide it in their rooms and backpacks.

There was usually almost no physical resemblance between tiny, pale, redheaded Bonnie and tall, olive-skinned, raven-haired Meredith, but at that moment, the suspicious, exasperated, yet affectionate expressions on their faces were almost identical.

"We promise we'll be careful," Meredith said gently, and Bonnie nodded. "But we're worried about you."

"I know," Elena said in a small voice. Silence stretched out between them and finally Meredith turned the light out again.

"We're here for you," Bonnie said in the darkness. "When you're ready."

"I know," Elena whispered again.

As she lay in the dark and listened to her friends' breathing gradually even out into the sounds of sleep, Elena turned and twisted from one side to the other, unable to get comfortable.

In Elena's own time, Meredith was miserable. She tried to cope, and she had Alaric helping her, and she almost never complained. But that didn't change the fact that Meredith had become a vampire, the one thing she never wanted to be.

Elena had to keep her out of this. Meredith deserved a chance at a normal life.

Knowing she had made the right decision, Elena finally dozed off into an uneasy sleep. When she woke, sunlight was shining brightly in the windows, and Meredith was standing at the foot of Elena's bed.

"Come on, sleepyhead," Meredith said lightly, jingling her car keys. "We've got to get to school."

"Okay, okay," Elena grumbled, sitting up and rubbing at her eyes. "I hardly slept, I couldn't—" She broke off in dismay, her words drying up.

Around her neck, Meredith was wearing the same deep red scarf she had worn last night. But something had changed while Elena slept. Below the scarf, she could see the edge of a deep purple-blue bruise. Elena knew exactly what it was, she had seen enough of them: a vampire bite.

*Damon Influenced her, once we were all asleep*, she thought, feeling dazed and nauseous. *Nowhere is safe.*

**22**

"We have to stop him," Elena insisted. "He's hurting the people I care about." She could hear her own voice rising hysterically, and she took a deep, shuddering breath, trying to calm down. The seemingly endless school day was finally over, but there were plenty of students still milling around. Enough people at their school already thought Stefan was an arsonist, no need to feed the rumors by making it sound like he was fighting with the queen of the school.

The *former* queen of the school, Elena amended mentally, noting another pair of eyes sliding over her suspiciously as two girls from her chemistry class walked by, heading between the trailers toward the parking lot. Everyone had noticed how different Elena was this year, and being seen arguing intensely in corners with Stefan was only pounding the nails in the coffin of her popularity.

Elena couldn't bring herself to care.

"Damon is coming after my friends," she said to Stefan, gripping his sleeve even more tightly. "It's all because of me. We have to protect them."

"I know," Stefan said. His leaf-green gaze was steady and reassuring. "Come back to the boardinghouse with me. We'll figure something out."

On the drive to the boardinghouse, Elena noticed how vividly red and yellow the leaves of the trees at the side of the road were getting. The long winding drive up to Mrs. Flowers' boardinghouse was lined with graceful birch trees whose golden leaves glowed like candles. Elena shivered. Halloween was coming soon. They were running out of time.

The old redbrick boardinghouse was dark and silent. Stefan unlocked one of the oak double doors and led Elena up the flight of stairs ahead of them. On the second-story landing, Elena turned automatically to the right, putting a hand on the knob of the door to the bedroom there.

Stefan went still as he stared at Elena. "How did you know which way to go?" he asked.

*Oops.* When Stefan had brought her here after Homecoming, they had gone in to his room via the balcony. Elena had never been up these stairs before. Not in this version of her life, anyway. "Just guessing," she said tentatively, and stood back to let him pass.

Stefan's lips thinned suspiciously, but he didn't say anything else. Elena meekly followed him through the bedroom and stood by as he opened what looked like a closet, revealing the flight of stairs that led up to his room.

Elena and Stefan stepped out of the stairway and into his dimly lit room. Stefan stopped dead, horror on his face. His room was destroyed. The heavy trunks that had stood between the windows were overturned, their lids smashed. Books cascaded from a broken bookcase, their covers dirty and torn as if they'd been stamped on. The blankets that had lain on Stefan's narrow bed were shredded. A cold breeze blew through the room from a smashed window at the far end.

"My God," Elena whispered. Damon must have done this.

The heavy mahogany dresser by the window was the only piece of furniture still standing, seemingly undamaged. Centered on its top stood a simple black iron box with a curving lid.

Stefan brushed past Elena and flung open the box. And then he froze, staring down into it.

"Stefan?" asked Elena softly after a moment. He didn't move or answer, and she wasn't sure if he had heard her. Stepping up beside him, she looked first at his face. It was even paler than usual, set in grim lines as if carved out of stone. His eyes, dark and stormy, stared unblinkingly down into the iron coffer, and Elena followed his gaze.

The box was empty.

Elena instantly understood. The iron box was where Stefan had kept his most precious things, the objects that recorded all his long, lonely history. His father's watch, carried by Stefan since the fifteenth century. The ivory dagger he had been given for his thirteenth birthday. Golden coins from his homeland. An agate-and-silver cup his mother, dead at Stefan's birth, had once treasured. Katherine's lapis lazuli ring. In a different time, a silk ribbon from Elena's hair.

All his treasures, gone. Elena looked back up at Stefan, but the words of sympathy she was about to say died on her lips. Stefan's face was no longer blank and cold. Instead, it was twisted in silent fury, his lips drawn back in a snarl.

He didn't look human, not anymore.

"I'll kill him," Stefan growled, his canines lengthening. "Damon destroys everything. For the *fun* of it."

Elena turned on her heel and raced down the stairs. "Mrs. Flowers!" she called as she hit the second floor. "Mrs. Flowers, where are you?" She stopped and listened, frustrated. Despite the many times she'd been in this house, she had never quite gotten a mental map of Mrs. Flowers' quarters, and the old witch woman wasn't especially likely to come when she was called.

"What is it, girl?" The voice was cold and clear, and Elena whipped around, her heart pounding. Stefan's landlady stood at the far end of the hall, a small, stooped figure, all in black.

"Mrs. Flowers," Elena said desperately, going toward her. "Someone was in Stefan's room. Did you see anyone?"

Mrs. Flowers was wise, and her magic was incredibly strong. But now the frail old lady looked at her warily, with no sign of recognition, and Elena remembered with dismay that, in this time, they had never met before.

"The message is for Stefan," Mrs. Flowers said clearly, in a slightly singsong voice, as if she was reciting from memory. Elena's heart sank further. Damon must have compelled her to let him in and deliver his message.

"I'm here," Stefan said from behind Elena. "Give me the message." He looked furious, still, but intensely weary. It was as if all the years, all the centuries, were catching up with him all at once.

"Damon says that you've taken something of his, and so he will take everything you have," Mrs. Flowers said, her face impassive. "Your precious things are his now."

"I never belonged to him," Elena said indignantly. "And I don't belong to Stefan. I'm not a *thing*."

But Mrs. Flowers, her message delivered, was already drifting back into her private part of the house, her long black shawl fluttering behind her.

Stefan's jaw was clenched tight, his fists balled and his green eyes dark. Elena didn't think she had ever seen him so angry, not in all the years she had known and loved him.

If, as Elena thought, Stefan and Damon carried each other's humanity … if it was the love between the brothers that was the key to Elena being able to change Damon and save them all …

If all these things were true, Elena couldn't help feeling like she might have already lost.

## 23

The next day, Elena hurried out of class and was the first one at her lunch table. The fire department had just declared that this wing of the school safe, and this was the first day they could eat in the cafeteria instead of outside. A smell of smoke still lingered here, though, and there were streaky gray stains of smoke on the walls and ceiling.

The morning had passed in a haze as she obediently went through the motions of being a high school student without hearing a word that was said. She thought that she might have taken a test in one of her classes, but she wasn't sure which class or what the test had asked. She couldn't think of anything that mattered less at this point in her life.

Maybe, she thought, staring down at her own nervously tapping fingers, her friends would be able to help after all. Elena was still determined not to tell them the truth about what Stefan and Damon were. They had all, Matt and Meredith especially, given up so much in Elena's real world. But, even without knowing all the facts, perhaps her friends could be her eyes and ears in Fell's Church. They could help her find Damon.

If she could just speak to Damon face-to-face, maybe Elena could talk some sense into him. She couldn't believe that he wouldn't come around. Deep down, Damon loved his brother. Elena was sure of it.

Caroline paused by the table. "All alone, Elena?" she asked, poisonously sweet.

Elena glanced up, and a sarcastic reply died on her lips. Around Caroline's pretty bronzed throat was wrapped a gauzy green scarf. Below it peeked out the edge of a tell-tale purpling bruise.

"What happened to your neck, Caroline?" she asked, her mouth dry.

Caroline sneered. "I don't know what you're talking about. Everything's wonderful." Turning on her heel, she walked away from Elena's table, her head held high.

Elena pressed a hand to her chest, trying to calm her pounding heart. First Meredith, then Caroline. Damon wanted Elena to know that he knew who the people around her were, that he could get to anyone that mattered to her.

"You okay, Elena?" Matt had stopped at her table. He grinned at her, solid and reassuring in his letterman's jacket.

Elena flinched. Beneath the collar of Matt's jacket, she could see a bite, angry purple with two darker marks in the center.

"What's that?" she asked, dazedly.

Matt raised his hand, brushing his fingers lightly across his neck just where the top of his shirt ended. For a moment, his face clouded, faintly puzzled, and then it cleared. "Everything's wonderful," he said slowly, then turned his back on Elena and walked away.

The same thing Caroline had said: *Everything's wonderful.* Damon had compelled them to say exactly those words and walk away. A hot flush of anger spread through Elena.

"It's only October, and I'm already so sick of school I could scream," Bonnie said, clattering her tray down on the table. "When am I really going to use Spanish anyway?"

"When you go to Mexico? Or talk to someone who speaks Spanish?" Meredith suggested dryly. "It might actually be one of the more useful subjects you take."

Bonnie clicked her tongue irritably as they sat down, but didn't argue. "Hey, Elena."

Elena greeted them distractedly. Meredith had another scarf looped around her neck, this one white with threads of sparkling silver woven through it. It covered the bite mark Elena had seen earlier, but she knew it was there.

Bonnie … Bonnie was fine. She was wearing a V-necked sweater, her slender white throat fully visible and completely unmarked. Elena looked carefully at Bonnie's wrists to see if Damon had fed from her veins there instead, but there was nothing to see but a braided bracelet and a thin gold watch.

"Elena, are you hearing a thing I say?" Meredith asked sharply. As Elena looked up, Meredith's expression of irritation softened to concern. "What's wrong?"

Elena straightened up and gave her a reassuring smile. "Nothing. I'm just distracted. What are we talking about?"

"We need to go to the warehouse at the lumberyard and finish planning out the Haunted House this afternoon," Meredith said patiently. "I know we still have the plans from last year, but this is our senior year. We should make it really special."

"Doing it there like we've always done will make things much easier. It would have been a huge hassle if we had to do it in the gym instead like the school board was talking about," Bonnie said. "It's, like, five hundred feet shorter. Yay for the fire, I guess."

The first time around—when Elena had been chairman of the decorating committee, instead of Meredith— the school board *had* made them set up the Haunted

House in the gym. They'd been worried by the attack on the homeless man under Wickery Bridge and thought everyone would be safer at school instead of at the lumberyard.

It was good that would be changing this time, she thought. If it were in a different place, were things less likely to happen the same way? Maybe.

Meredith pulled out her planning notebook, and she and Bonnie were quickly absorbed in the pictures and sketches from the previous year's Haunted House. Elena's eyes wandered back to Bonnie's unmarked throat.

It just didn't make *sense*, she thought. If Damon was being thorough enough to go after everyone important to Elena—and Caroline was important to her, Elena admitted to herself, even if they didn't like each other—then why hadn't he fed from Bonnie?

Maybe he just hadn't gotten around to it yet.

"I think we should have druids," Bonnie was saying.

"Actually, that's not a bad idea—" Meredith said, and Elena interrupted.

"Bonnie, have you seen Damon lately?" she asked abruptly. "The guy who brought me to school that day?" *Why* had he not bitten Bonnie?

"The one who saw her kissing Stefan," Meredith said unhelpfully.

Bonnie flushed, right up to her hairline, and shifted uncomfortably in her seat. "I meant to tell you," she blurted. "Only it was really weird, and I didn't want you to feel bad."

"What do you mean?"

"I was at the grocery store the other night picking up milk for my mom, and he came up and started talking to me." Bonnie looked down, pushing her hair shyly behind her ear. "He was looking into my eyes and saying, just, really weird stuff. Like that I *wanted to be close to him*. I didn't want to tell you because it felt like he was hitting on me." She glanced up at Elena, looking guilty. "I didn't do anything, I swear."

"I believe you," Elena said soothingly, trying to think. Why would Damon have let Bonnie go? It certainly sounded like he had started to compel her; why would he have changed his mind?

Bonnie and Damon had always had a special bond. He called her his redbird, and was protective, treating her almost like a little sister. But, no, that wasn't true *here*. Damon didn't know Bonnie well enough to care about her, not yet.

Elena looked at Bonnie's white throat again, at her slender wrists, checking once more for bites and bruises she knew she wasn't going to find.

Bonnie's wrists ... Elena leaned forward, frowning. The narrow woven bracelet around Bonnie's left wrist was made of thin strips of leather and bits of colored thread and small silver beads. And strands of some kind of plant. Was it *vervain*?

"Where'd you get that bracelet?" Elena asked her.

Bonnie stretched her left arm out to look at it. "I know, it's kind of ugly, isn't it? My grandmother gave it to me this summer, though, and she told me never to take it off. It's supposed to protect me against all kinds of things."

"Because she and your cousin and you are all psychic." Meredith said teasingly.

Bonnie shrugged. "It's all about the druids. Which is why we should have them in the Haunted House. For one thing, they did human sacrifice, and we could have, like, a standing stone and a big knife ... Elena? Where are you going?"

Elena wasn't listening anymore. Without even thinking about it, she stood up from the table and walked out first the cafeteria doors and then the doors of the school. No one stopped her as she strode between the temporary trailer classrooms and through the parking lot.

She felt hot and angry, fuming as she stomped down the sidewalk away from the school. Damon had attacked Meredith. Matt. Even Caroline. And he'd tried to feed on Bonnie as well.

Bonnie was safe. For now. As long as she didn't take that bracelet off and Damon didn't decide that just grabbing her and feeding off her without first compelling her was just as good.

Elena had kissed Stefan *once*. Once. And her friends had had nothing to do with it.

She was tired of playing games.

When she reached the graveyard, Elena hesitated for a moment, staring through the fence. The day was cloudy, and the cemetery looked gray and gloomy. Beyond the ruined church, she could see the branches of the uprooted tree, pointing skyward.

As she passed through the gate, a cold wind began to blow, whistling in Elena's ears and whipping her hair against her face. She turned toward the well-kept, modern part of the cemetery with its neat rows of granite and marble tombstones. For this confrontation, Elena instinctively felt that it would be comforting to have her parents nearby.

The cemetery was empty and still. As Elena crossed it, the wind came with her, piles of dry leaves rising up into the air as she passed. She stopped by her parents' grave and rested a hand on the cool gray granite of their stone, gathering her strength. "Help me, Mom and Dad," she murmured. Anger was still simmering inside her, black and hot.

Elena spun around, searching between the headstones. She knew he was there, somewhere, watching her. It didn't matter that the bond between them had been severed, she could *feel* him.

She gathered her breath and shouted, into the wind. *"Damon!"*

Nothing. A memory of doing this once before had her turning on the spot, looking over her own shoulder, only to see no one there.

"Damon!" she shouted again. "I know you're there!"

Icy wind blew straight into Elena's face, making her flinch. When she opened her eyes, she found herself staring across the graveyard at a grove of beech trees, their leaves bright yellow and red against the grayness of the sky. Something dark moved in the shadows between their trunks.

Elena blinked. The blackness was coming closer, its shape resolving into a black-clad figure. Golden leaves blew around him, parting as he stepped forward to the edge of the grove, and his pale features became clearer.

Damon, of course.

He stayed where he was, watching Elena calmly as she hurried toward him. She almost slipped in the grass, catching herself against a tombstone, and heat rose in her cheeks. She didn't want to seem vulnerable in front of Damon. Whatever game he was playing, she would need all the advantages she could get.

"What do you think you're doing?" she snapped when she reached him, slightly out of breath.

Damon flashed her a bright, insincere smile. "I came when you called, Princess," he said. "I could ask you the same thing. Everything's wonderful." He hissed the words, his lips curling into a cruel smile, the same words he'd primed Matt and Caroline and probably Meredith with, and her anger flared up, hot inside her. Elena's hand flew out and she slapped Damon hard across the face.

Her hand stung with the force of the blow, and Damon's cheek reddened, but he was still smiling. "Don't push me too hard, Elena," he said softly. "I've been kinder than you deserve."

"You've been feeding on my friends," she said, her voice shaking.

Damon's eyes glittered, so black she couldn't tell the iris from the pupil. "Not just feeding on them, Elena. I've got big plans."

Elena went cold inside. "What do you mean?"

Damon's smile disappeared. "The way I fell for you so quickly … It made me realize how lonely I must be."

Elena's heart thumped hard. Damon didn't do vulnerable, didn't admit to having emotions. Could this be a *good* thing?

But Damon went on, lightly. "And so, I decided what I needed were some protégés."

"You can't do that," Elena said. Damon had never turned anyone into a vampire, never, to her knowledge, even offered to turn anyone except Elena herself. He wasn't looking for companionship; this was pure spite.

"Oh, I can," Damon said. "I think Halloween will be an appropriate day to do it, don't you? It's a very American holiday, of course, but I've always liked costumes. Ghosts and ghasts and all sorts of ghoulies."

"Damon," Elena said. *"Don't."*

She could hear the pleading tone in her own voice, and so could Damon. His smile reappeared, flashing sharp and bright and quickly disappearing again.

"They'll thank me," he said softly, "when they realize they'll be young and beautiful forever." His eyes ran over her, pausing on the bite mark Stefan had left low on her throat. When he spoke again, his voice was laced with bitterness. "I'd invite you to join us, Elena, but you'll have Stefan for that."

Elena stepped closer. "I'm not with Stefan," she said, her words tumbling over one another. "I was never with Stefan, Damon. We kissed *once*, that's it, and that was a mistake. The only reason he fed on me was so that we could get out of the tomb *you* locked us into."

Damon's mouth tightened. He looked as disturbingly handsome as ever, but there was something bitter and distrustful in his face. "I'll see you on Halloween, Elena," he said, and then he was gone.

Elena stood alone in the cemetery, surrounded by strangers' graves.

She swallowed once, hard, and pressed the heels of her hands against her eyes for a moment.

Damon wanted to change Matt, Meredith, and Caroline—and who knew who else—into vampires on Halloween. Elena had to stop him. And she needed to stop him from killing Mr. Tanner that same night. She didn't know how she was going to do it alone.

Stefan was clever and strong. If he drank her blood, he'd have more Power, maybe enough to stop Damon.

But no. Elena discarded the idea as swiftly as it had come to her. Stefan had been so angry at Damon when he realized Damon had stolen his treasures. All the conflict, all the resentment that had lain between the brothers since the days of Katherine, 500 years before, had simmered behind Stefan's green eyes, ready to boil over. If she brought him up against Damon now, Stefan might lose his head and attack. And then there was a good chance that Damon might kill him.

But thinking of the brothers' shared past had given Elena an idea. Straightening her sweater and squaring her shoulders, she turned and began walking back toward school, leaves crunching beneath her feet.

She needed magic.

\* \* \*

Despite all that had happened since she left the cafeteria, Elena was only a few minutes late for history class. Murmuring an apology to the teacher, she ignored the curious gazes of her classmates. Pulling a sheet of loose-leaf paper out of her backpack, she bent her head over her desk and wrote a note.

*SOS. I need your help. Meet me at your house after school. TELL NO ONE!!!*

Folding the note and passing it to a girl to her right, Elena jerked her head toward Bonnie's front-row seat, and the girl obediently passed it forward. Elena watched as Bonnie glanced up to make sure Mr. Tanner's eyes were elsewhere, unfolded the note, read it, and then scribbled a reply.

When it came back to Elena, Bonnie's rounded handwriting read,

*Can't! We have to go to the warehouse to plan the Haunted House, remember? Meredith would kill us!!!*

Mr. Tanner's attention was fixed on a boy answering a question on the other side of the room, and Elena took the chance to grimace appealingly at Bonnie, trying to express urgency in her face. Bonnie, twisted around in her seat, shook her head.

Elena quickly wrote another note and passed it back up to Bonnie.

*You have to meet me. I have so much to tell you.*
*Bonnie, you're a witch.*

## 24

"Are you serious about all this?" Bonnie asked. "I'm not going to be mad if you were kidding, Elena." She hefted one of the bags Mrs. Flowers had given them over her shoulder and stepped carefully over a broken gravestone.

Elena had told Bonnie everything. About Stefan and Damon, about coming here from a possible future. About how Bonnie would grow into one of the most powerful witches Elena had ever met. How much Elena needed her help.

Telling Bonnie was the only thing she could think of to do. Matt and Meredith had been hurt too much by their association with the supernatural to bring them into this. Stefan would have been the worst person imaginable to pit against Damon right now.

But Bonnie? In the future, Bonnie was happy. And she was amazingly full of Power. If only they could tap into that Power now, use Bonnie's magic even though she was completely untrained, Bonnie could be a true asset.

It hadn't been easy. At first, Bonnie had shaken her head, her large brown eyes wide, and backed away from Elena nervously. The step from saying she was psychic and could read palms to being told she was a budding witch had almost been too much for her. Even now, she was sneaking dubious, worried glances out of the corner of her eye at Elena. But she was here. She wasn't running away.

Mrs. Flowers had been a surprisingly huge help. She had stood in the doorway of her big old house, listening silently as Elena stumbled through an explanation that really explained nothing. It boiled down to the fact that they knew Mrs. Flowers was a witch, and that they needed help opening something.

"And protecting ourselves," Elena had tossed in, almost as an afterthought.

Mrs. Flowers sharp eyes examined first Elena, then Bonnie. After a while, she had simply turned and walked away.

"Uh," Bonnie had said, peering down the dark hall after the old woman. "Are we supposed to follow her?"

Despite everything, Elena could feel a smile curling at the edges of her lips. "It's just the way she is. She'll come back."

They'd waited what felt like forever at Mrs. Flowers's door, long enough that Bonnie began casting dubious looks at Elena again and Elena began to worry about what she would do if Stefan came home and saw them there.

But Mrs. Flowers had returned eventually, carrying two duffle bags, and spoke for the first time since Elena had asked her for help. "You'll find things labeled in there, dear. And good luck getting back where you belong."

"Thank you—" Elena began to say, but the heavy doors were already swinging shut, leaving Elena and Bonnie on the doorstep. She frowned, confused. How had Mrs. Flowers known this wasn't where Elena belonged?

"Pretty weird," Bonnie had said, shaking her head. But she had actually seemed slightly less freaked out after that, as if she found it comforting that Elena wasn't the only possibly crazy person around.

Now they crossed the older part of the graveyard, staggering a little under the weight of the duffle bags Mrs. Flowers had given them. Bonnie hesitated in the empty hole that had once been the doorway of the ruined church.

"Are we allowed in here?" she asked. "Is it safe?"

"Probably not," Elena told her, "but we have to go in. Please, Bonnie."

Most of the roof had fallen in and late afternoon sunlight streamed through the holes above them, illuminating piles of rubble. Three walls still stood, but the fourth was knee-high, and Elena could see the far end of the graveyard through it. The uprooted tree, its branches brushing the walls of the small mausoleum Damon had trapped her and Stefan in, still lay there in ruins.

At the side of the church was the tomb of Thomas and Honoria Fell, a large stone box, heavy marble figures carved on its lid. Elena walked over to gaze down on the founders of Fell's Church, lying with hands folded across their chests, their eyes closed. Elena brushed her fingers across Honoria's cold marble cheek, taking comfort from the face of the lady who had guarded Fell's Church for so long. Her ghost hadn't appeared this time. Did that mean she trusted Elena to handle the situation? Or was something preventing her from coming?

"Okay," Elena said, all business, as she swung around to face Bonnie. "We have to get the tomb open."

Bonnie's eyes rounded. "Are you kidding me?" she asked. "That's what you want to open? Elena, it's got to weigh about a thousand pounds. We can't open that with herbs and candles. You need a bulldozer or something."

"We can," Elena said steadily. "You have the Power, Bonnie."

"Even if we could"—Bonnie's voice wobbled—"what would be the point? Elena, there are *dead people* in that thing."

"No," Elena said, her eyes fixed thoughtfully on the gray stone box. "It's not really a grave. It's a passageway."

They rummaged through the duffle bags. "Here," Elena said, pulling out two little red silk bags, each on a long loop of cord. "Mrs. Flowers gave us sachets for protection. Put it around your neck." The tiny bag was round and fat with herbs, fitting comfortably in the palm of Elena's hand.

"What's in them?" At Elena's shrug, Bonnie sniffed the sachet before stringing it around her neck. "Smells good, anyway."

There were small jars of herbs, labeled in Mrs. Flowers' crabbed, almost illegible handwriting. "It says these are cowslips," Elena said, making out the label on a jar of small dried yellow flowers, several blossoms on each stem. "According to the label, they're good for unlocking."

Bonnie leaned against her and looked down at the jar in Elena's hand. "Okay. So what do we do with them?"

Elena stared at her. *What would Bonnie, my Bonnie, do?* She tried to think.

"Well, when you're doing a spell that uses herbs, you usually scatter them around what you're working on," she said. "Or you burn them."

"Right. Well, I'd rather not set the church on fire, so let's try scattering them," Bonnie said dryly.

As well as the cowslips, there were jars of prickly dried evergreen needles and dried berries labeled JUNIPER—FOR SPELLCASTING and an herb Elena recognized as rosemary, the label of which claimed it was used for luck and power. Mrs. Flowers had given them several small jars of each, so there was more than enough to strew thoroughly over the lid of the tomb and in a circle around it.

*Help us*, Elena thought fervently as she sprinkled rosemary over Honoria Fell's grave. *If this works, we'll be protecting Fell's Church. Just like you wanted.*

"Now what?" Bonnie asked, when they'd scattered all the herbs. "There are candles in the other bag, and matches. And a flashlight. And, yikes, a knife."

There were twelve candles, four each of black, white, and red. Mrs. Flowers hadn't included any kind of note to tell them what the colors meant or what exactly to do with them, so Elena, hoping she was doing the right thing, decided to put them in a circle, colors alternating, around the tomb, outside the circle of herbs.

"And what do we do next?" Bonnie asked, watching as Elena lit the last candle.

"I'm not sure," Elena told her, dripping a pool of candle wax on the floor and carefully sticking the candle upright in it. "Usually, you say something, maybe just saying what you want to happen, and it looks like you're concentrating."

Bonnie's eyebrows shot up. "So the next step is that I say 'open' and *think really hard*? Elena, I'm not sure this is going to work."

"Try it," Elena said hopefully.

Bonnie frowned at the tomb. The flames of the candles danced, reflected in her eyes. "Open," she said firmly.

Nothing happened.

"Open. I command you to open." Bonnie said, more doubtfully, and closed her eyes, scrunching her forehead in concentration. Still, nothing changed.

Bonnie's eyes opened and she huffed in frustration. "This is ridiculous."

"Wait." Elena thought of the knife, still in the bag. "Sometimes, you use blood. You say it's important, that it's one of the strongest ingredients you can use in a spell. Because it's vitality, it's life in its most basic form." She hurried toward the bag and felt inside. The knife was more like a small dagger, its blade pure silver and its handle some kind of bone.

Bonnie hesitated, biting her lip, and then nodded. She came to stand beside Elena, her eyes fixed on the knife.

"I'll go first, okay?" Elena said. She made a short, shallow cut on the inside of her own arm, hissing a little at the stinging pain. Turning her arm, she let the blood drip across Honoria and Thomas Fell's effigies. Splotches of her blood stained their lips, the lids of their closed eyes. Blood dripped on Honoria's neck and trickled down, making it look as if she'd been a vampire's feast.

*Please,* Elena thought, breathing hard. *Please let us in.* She wasn't sure who she was begging: Honoria Fell; the mysterious Powers that filled the universe; the Celestial Guardians; or Katherine, down below the church. Whoever was listening, she supposed. Whoever would help her.

Bonnie, white-faced but resolute, held out her own arm, and Elena ran the blade quickly across it, watching the blood spill out and over Bonnie's porcelain-white skin. More blood spattered over Honoria and Thomas's stone torsos and their folded hands.

"Draw on your Power, Bonnie," Elena said softly. "It's there. I've seen it. Pull it out of the earth under your feet and the plants growing all around us. Take it from the dead; they're right here with us."

Bonnie's face tightened with concentration, her fine bones becoming more defined beneath her skin. The candle flames flickered, all at once, as if a wind had passed through the ruined church.

Elena wasn't a Guardian here, and she didn't have those Powers anymore. But she could remember what it had felt like when she and Bonnie worked together, their auras combining, feeding her Power into Bonnie's. She tried to find that feeling, pushing out, trying to let Bonnie take whatever might help her. Her hand found Bonnie's smaller one, and Bonnie twined their fingers together and squeezed hard.

All at once, the candles all went out. With a huge, grating cracking noise, the top of the stone tomb split in half, one side falling heavily to the flagstones of the floor.

Elena peered down. As she had expected, there was no grave beneath the stone. Instead of bones, she was looking down into the dark opening of a vault. In the stone wall below her were driven iron rungs, like a ladder.

"Wow." Bonnie said next to her. She was pale, but her eyes were shining with excitement. "I can't believe that worked. I *can't* ..." She closed her mouth, then cleared her throat and lifted her chin bravely. "What now?"

"Now you go home," Elena said. She looked nervously out the broken wall of the church. It was still daylight, but the sun was sinking low. She pulled the flashlight out of the bag and tucked it into her back pocket. "I'm sorry, Bonnie, and *thank you*, thank you so much. But the next part I have to do by myself. And I'm not sure if it's safe for you up here. Please go home before it gets dark."

"If it's not safe for me, it's not safe for you," Bonnie said stubbornly. "At least I can watch your back."

Elena squeezed her friend's hand. "Please, Bonnie," she begged again. "I can't do what I have to do if I'm worrying about you. I promise I'll be okay."

She knew she had no way of guaranteeing that, but Bonnie's shoulders slumped in acceptance. "Be careful, Elena," she said. "Call me as soon as you get home."

"Okay." Elena watched as Bonnie picked up the duffle bags with their depleted jars of herbs and left the church, casting worried glances back at Elena over her shoulder.

Once Bonnie's small, upright figure was out of sight, Elena took a deep breath. There was an icy breeze coming from the opening in the tomb, and it smelled like earth and cold stone that never saw the light.

Steeling herself, she swung her legs over the edge of the tomb, took hold of an iron rung, and began to climb down into the vault beneath the church.

lena climbed down into darkness, the iron rungs cold in her hands. By the time her feet hit the stone floor at the bottom of the ladder, she was in total blackness. Pulling the flashlight from her back pocket, she flicked it on and ran the beam of light over her surroundings.

The opening of the crypt was just as Elena remembered it. Smooth stone walls held heavy carved candelabras, some with the remains of candles still in them. Near Elena was an ornate wrought-iron gate. Pushing the gate open, Elena walked forward with a slow, steady tread, trying to calm her hammering heart.

The last time she had been here, she'd been a vampire, and she'd had Damon and Stefan both with her, as well as her human friends. More important, that time she hadn't known what she was getting into. Only that she had been led down here, and that something terrible lurked, just out of sight.

Now Elena knew exactly what was down here.

Her steady footsteps echoed against the stone floor, their sounds only emphasizing how silent it was. Elena could easily believe that no one else had been down here for more than a hundred years. No one else alive, anyway.

Beyond the gate, the beam of the flashlight caught on pale, familiar marble features. A tomb, the twin of the one up in the church. The stone lid here had been broken in two also, and the pieces flung across the crypt. Fragile human bones were splintered and strewn sticklike across the floor. One crunched beneath Elena's feet as she approached, making her wince guiltily.

She had hoped that, since Katherine hadn't appeared in Fell's Church, hadn't sent disturbing dreams to torment Elena, it meant she wasn't so filled with rage in this time. But the violence with which the tomb had been desecrated seemed to prove that Katherine was as furious and destructive as she had ever been.

Elena turned the thin wavering beam of the flashlight to the wall beyond the Fells' tomb. There, as she'd known there would be, lay a gaping hole in the stone wall, as if the stones had been ripped away. From it, a long black tunnel led deep into the earth beyond.

Elena licked her lips nervously. Resting her hands on the cold moist dirt at the edge of the tunnel, she peered into it. "Katherine?" she said questioningly. Her voice came out softer and shakier than she had meant it to, and she cleared her throat and called again. *"Katherine!"*

Straining her eyes to see into the darkness, Elena waited.

Nothing. No sound of footfalls, nothing white coming swiftly toward her. No sense of something huge and dangerous rushing at her.

"Katherine!" she called again. "I have secrets to tell you!" That might bring her if anything would; Katherine von Swartzchild, first love of Damon and Stefan, the one who had made them vampires and turned them against each other was nothing if not curious and eager for information. That was why she had followed Stefan and Damon here, why she had spied on Elena.

Elena waited, watching and listening. Still nothing. She felt her shoulders sag. Without Katherine, she didn't have a plan at all.

How long should she wait? Elena pictured herself sitting against the wall, surrounded by the Fell's broken bones, waiting for Katherine, growing colder and colder as the light of the flashlight dimmed. Elena shuddered. No, she wouldn't stay here.

She turned to go, and the beam of the flashlight landed on Katherine, standing only a few feet behind her. Elena jumped backward with a strained yelp, her light skittering wildly across the crypt.

Katherine looked so much like Elena that it knocked Elena breathless, even now. Her golden hair was perhaps a shade lighter and a few inches longer, her eyes a slightly different blue. Her figure was thinner and more fragile than Elena's: Girls of her time and class had been expected to sit and embroider, not run and play.

But the delicate curve of Katherine's brow, her long golden lashes, her pale skin, the shape of her features— they were all as familiar to Elena as looking in a mirror. Unlike Elena, who was dressed in jeans and a sweater, Katherine wore a long, gauzy white dress. It would have made her look innocent, if it weren't for the brownish-red streaks across the front, as if Katherine had absent-mind-edly wiped bloody hands on it.

"Hello, pretty little girl, my sweet reflection," Katherine said, almost crooning.

Elena swallowed nervously. "I need your help."

Katherine came closer, touching Elena's hair, running cold fingers across her face. "You're a nasty, greedy girl," she said sharply. "You want both my boys."

"You wanted them, too," Elena snapped, not bothering to deny it. Katherine smiled, her teeth disturbingly sharp.

"Of course I did," she said. "But they're mine. They've always been mine. You should have left them alone."

"I *am* going to leave them alone from now on," Elena said. "I promise. I just want them to be brothers. I want them to be happy. You did too once."

Katherine had, Elena knew, let both brothers drink her blood, promised them each eternal life with the secret idea that they would love each other, that the three of them could be a happy family, together forever. When they had rejected the idea of sharing her, she faked her own death, sure their mutual grief would bring them together.

She'd been a fool. Damon and Stefan had loathed each other already, distanced by their competition for their father's love, by their roles as the good and bad sons. Jealousy over Katherine had only heightened their dislike, and their anger and grief at her death had ripened it into hatred.

Katherine had expected Stefan and Damon to turn to each other, but instead they had turned *on* each other, swords in hand. Each murdered at his brother's hand, they'd died with Katherine's blood in their systems, and risen again, vampires, cursed forever.

"They don't want to be happy." Katherine's eyes widened with remembered hurt, and for a moment, Elena saw the fragile, naïve girl who had destroyed Damon and

Stefan with a mistaken idea of romance. "I gave them a gift. I gave them life forever, and they didn't care. I told them to take care of each other, in my memory, but they wouldn't listen. They threw everything I'd given them away."

"But maybe it's not too late," Elena said. "Maybe if they knew you were alive, they could forgive each other."

Katherine's eyes narrowed angrily, her lips curling into a sulky pout. "I don't want them to forgive each other," she said in a childish voice. Then she began to smile, an unpleasant, hungry smile. "You, on the other hand ..." She stroked Elena's cheeks. Her hands were terribly cold, and they smelled of the earth around them. Elena shivered. "We look so much alike," Katherine said musingly. "I should make you like me. We could travel together. It would be such fun. Everyone would think we were sisters."

There was something wistful in Katherine's eyes as her hand shifted to run through Elena's hair, pulling a little at the long strands. Maybe family was what Katherine needed. She'd lost her father when she'd lost the Salvatores and fled Italy. Would knowing she had other family make a difference to Katherine?

"We are sisters," she said, and Katherine's hand pulled away.

"I don't know what you mean, little one," Katherine said. "You're no sister of mine."

Elena swallowed, feeling the dry click of her throat. "We really are. My mother—your mother—was an immortal. A Celestial Guardian. She left you to keep you safe. And when, hundreds of years later, she tried to keep me safe, the other Guardians killed her."

Katherine's mouth tightened into an angry line. "That doesn't make any sense. My mother died when I was a baby."

"No, it's true," Elena said simply. There was nothing but hostility in Katherine's face, but Elena pushed on. "I ask you, as your own flesh and blood, to help me. You wanted to be the one to bring Stefan and Damon together, and you still can be. They need you, Katherine. Five hundred years, and they've never stopped loving you. It's torn them apart."

Katherine's face was blank and cold. "They deserve to suffer." She squeezed her fists tightly, slamming her arms down at her sides. "They'll suffer if I kill you. Or if I take you with me."

"No." Elena took Katherine's cold, muddy arm, her heart pounding. "They've suffered all along. You can *save* them this time. You're the only one who can."

Hissing, Katherine pulled away. With a rattling noise, the crypt began to shake around them. Despite herself,

Elena shrieked as the lid to the tomb fell to the floor with a crash, Honoria Fell's face cracking. Another tremor had Elena stumbling and grabbing onto the stone wall to keep from falling.

"Stop it!" she demanded, glaring at Katherine. The other girl stood stock-still, her pale face tilted up as if she could see through the dirt and stone to the ruined church above. From high above, Elena heard a heavy thud, and Katherine's lips curled in a joyless smile.

Elena ran. Her heart pounding, she shoved through the half-open gate and down the long dark corridor, her flashlight swinging wildly. She didn't look back, but her nerves were on edge, listening for a footstep, waiting for Katherine's inhumanly strong hands to clamp down upon her shoulders and drag Elena back.

Katherine could kill her, could turn Elena into a vampire if she wanted to, and there was nothing Elena would be able to do about it. Why had Elena tried to reason with her?

Grabbing hold of the iron rungs set in the wall, Elena began to pull herself up as fast as she could, her breath coming fast and anxious. The crypt had stopped shaking, for now, but her hands, sweaty with nerves, still slipped as she climbed. Partway up, she lost her grip on the flashlight and it fell, crashing into the stones below and going out, leaving Elena in darkness. Far above was the faintly lit rectangle of the tomb in the church, and Elena kept climbing toward it as fast as she could, holding tightly onto the rungs.

At last Elena reached the top and scrambled out through the Fells' tomb, gulping deep breaths of the cold fresh air. Once she was standing on the floor of the old church, she dared to glance down into the crypt below.

There was nothing there, no white-clad figure following her. But that proved nothing. Katherine could take many forms, and she was much, much faster than Elena. Elena's best chance, she thought, would be to cross Wickery Bridge and head home as quickly as she could. Katherine was powerful enough that she had trouble crossing running water.

The sun had set and night had fallen while Elena was down in the crypt. *Terrific*, she thought, *a cemetery after dark without a flashlight and a vampire on my heels. This was a truly genius idea, Elena Gilbert.*

She stumbled over what seemed to be every tombstone in the long grass of the older part of the graveyard, once falling hard enough to skin the palms of her hands. Elena scrambled up and hurried on, finding her way by the light of the half-moon above her.

Once she reached the road outside the cemetery, the tight ball of anxiety in Elena's chest relaxed a little. Not much farther until she could cross the bridge and then head back home. She'd have to go back to her own house. Aunt Judith had called someone to fix the window and insisted on moving back home. At least it was closer than Meredith's, but Elena didn't know how to keep them safe from Damon. Perhaps now that he was focusing on her friends, he would leave Elena's family alone.

Just before the bridge, a white-clad figure barred Elena's path. Katherine's pale gold hair whipped around her in the wind.

Elena glanced back over her shoulder. There was no point in running. Katherine was a thousand times faster than Elena, and the only thing that would hinder her— running water—was on the *other* side of her.

For a moment, Elena thought of begging for mercy. But she knew Katherine well enough to know that wouldn't do any good. Whatever Katherine decided to do, she would do.

*Might as well go out fighting.* Elena tossed her head back and marched straight up to Katherine. "What do you want?" she asked.

Katherine's cold blue eyes regarded Elena for a long moment. Finally, she spoke. "You think that I can save them? I'll do as you ask, little mirror. I will let Damon and Stefan know that I still live."

"Oh." Maybe Elena's pleading had done some good after all. "Thank you."

Katherine frowned at her crossly. For a moment, her voice sounded young, a hurt child's, but her eyes seemed terribly old. "There's no happy ending in this for either of us. I hope you know that," she said. "I've lived this once already. I know what it's like to love them both, and to lose them."

eavy clouds loomed overhead, and the air seemed ominously electric, on the verge of a storm. Outside the Haunted House appeared a devilishly masked mannequin, its black clothing flapping in the wind and giving an appropriately nightmarish ambiance to this Halloween night.

Stefan and Elena stopped outside the Haunted House. Stefan's face was drawn tight, and Elena felt sick and anxious. Pulling up the hood of her Red Riding Hood costume, she carefully covered her distinctive golden hair.

"This is the night Damon said he was going to turn Meredith and Matt and Caroline into vampires," she whispered to Stefan. "He has to be here. They're all here, and there's so much confusion, it will be easy for him."

Stefan nodded grimly. Looking up at him, Elena couldn't help the little clench her heart gave. He looked so good in his tuxedo and cape, elegant and completely natural. A debonair vampire costume, what else? And people thought Stefan didn't have a sense of humor.

She hadn't been completely honest with him. For her plan to work, for the brothers to forgive each other, Katherine's revelation that they hadn't caused her death had to come as a surprise. So she had told him only that they needed to protect her friends from Damon.

"We'll mingle with the crowd and keep an eye out for him," she said as they approached the Haunted House entrance. "If you hang out in the Torture Room, that might be a good place. It shouldn't be too crowded; it's off the main path and it's mostly dummies, not people in costume. It's the kind of place Damon would be likely to take someone if he wanted to be alone."

Despite Elena's defection from the Haunted House committee—which Meredith had only reluctantly forgiven her for—and Bonnie's missing most of the all-important planning stage, Meredith and the rest of her decorating committee had done an amazing job on the Haunted House. It looked nightmarishly creepy, the entrance enthusiastically draped in spider webs and handprints made with fake blood.

Now everything was in chaos as the seniors rushed to get the last pieces in place before the paying public was allowed in. Elena and Stefan ducked through the crowd and made their way along the twisting route of the tour.

Outside the Torture Chamber, Elena squeezed Stefan's hand. "This is it," she said. "Good luck."

"I will protect them if I can, Elena," Stefan told her, and slipped through the doorway to hide inside among the torture implements.

Elena went on, glancing in at the different sets as she passed. The Alien Encounter Room was already dark, lit only with phosphorescent paint, and zombies milled around the Living Dead Room, adjusting one another's makeup.

The Druid Room was near the back of the warehouse, and Elena frowned. If she'd had time to really participate in the committee, maybe she could have made it more central, so that it would be more difficult for Damon to feed from—and kill—Mr. Tanner.

*Love is powerful*, Mylea had said, but should Elena have paid more attention to logistics and less to changing Damon's heart? She should have made it *impossible* for Damon to kill Mr. Tanner instead of hoping she could make him not want to.

She swallowed hard. This was the right way to go. If she couldn't change the relationship between the brothers, surely it was only a matter of time before Damon killed again. She could only hope that Katherine would pull through, for all their sakes. If it didn't work, maybe there was never any hope for Elena's mission.

And there Mr. Tanner was, upright and indignant, arguing with white-robed Bonnie in front of a cardboard Stonehenge. "But you've *got* to wear the blood," she was saying pleadingly. "It's part of the scene; you're a sacrifice."

"Wearing these ridiculous robes is bad enough," Mr. Tanner told her. "No one informed me I was going to have to smear syrup all over myself."

"It doesn't really get on *you*," Bonnie argued, but Elena had heard enough for now. She remembered this argument. She'd joined in the first time, trying to convince Mr. Tanner to cooperate, and then Stefan had finally compelled him. But Meredith, a witch in a tight black dress, was already approaching, and Elena realized she had faith that Meredith's logic and persistence would be just as effective as Stefan's Power had been.

Both Bonnie and Meredith were focused on Mr. Tanner, not even noticing Elena, and she hesitated, watching them. Meredith was talking softly and reasonably to Mr. Tanner while Bonnie looked harried but amused, a smile lurking at the edges of her mouth.

Elena's heart ached with how much she loved them. Memories came rushing back to her: Meredith telling ghost stories at their junior high sleepovers, Bonnie's face bright over her ninth birthday cake, the focused frown Meredith wore as she studied, the shine of Bonnie's eyes on her wedding day. Damon wanted to *change* them, destroy their lives, make them unaging killers. She had to stop him.

It was almost time for the Haunted House to open. Time to look for Damon.

The Haunted House was like a maze this time, Elena realized. The warehouse was bigger than the school gym had been, and Meredith had filled the space with many more horrors than they'd been able to fit in the school gym the first time this Halloween had happened, when Elena had been in charge. Elena cut through the Séance Room and the Deaths from History Room, where she spotted Caroline, a nubile Egyptian priestess in a linen shift that left very little to the imagination, talking to Tyler in his werewolf costume. *One potential victim*, she thought, and looked for the others. She would have to keep them all safe.

Slipping between the temporary partitions, Elena cut through the Spider Room, where she had to push her way through dangling rubber spiders. She found Meredith and Bonnie again, and followed as they hurried back toward the entrance, ready to lead customers through the house. Outside the entrance to the fun house, she finally identified Matt, who had taken the head of his own werewolf costume off. *Everyone in place*, she thought, and glanced automatically toward the Torture Chamber.

The last of the seniors were getting in position. The doors were about to open. "Bonnie," Elena said softly, coming up next to her.

Bonnie jumped a little. "Elena," she said. She looked curiously at Elena's costume. "I thought you were going to wear that Renaissance dress your aunt had made for you."

"No, I lent that to someone else," Elena told her. "Bonnie, can you do me a favor? Damon's going to come here, dressed as the Grim Reaper. Be nice to him, okay? Don't let on that you recognize him if you can help it, and steer him toward the Torture Chamber. I'll take it from there."

Bonnie paled, but she nodded. "I'll try," she said, and lowered her voice to a whisper. "What if he tries to bite me, Elena?"

Elena slipped an arm around her friend's shoulders. "I don't think he will, at least not here," she said comfortingly. "You've got your bracelet and Mrs. Flowers's sachet, so he can't Influence you, and I don't think he'll try anything with this many people around. If he does, just scream as loudly as you can."

Bonnie didn't seem terribly comforted, but she nodded again and squared her shoulders. For a moment, she looked to Elena like a young soldier heading into battle. Frightened, but firmly determined to face down death if necessary. Suddenly filled with affection, Elena hugged her friend tightly. "It'll be all right," she breathed in Bonnie's ear. "I promise." Something twisted inside her, and she hoped, fervently, that she would be able to keep the promise.

A voice sounded through the warehouse. "Okay, they're about to let in the line. Cut the lights, Ed!" Gloom fell, and, with an audible click, somebody started the recorded sounds of groans and maniacal laughter, so that they resounded through the Haunted House. Letting go of Bonnie, Elena headed for her own chosen spot as the doors opened to let in the crowd.

It took a long time for Damon to appear. From her hiding place behind a particularly gruesome-looking plastic apparatus and agonized dummy in the Torture Room, Elena listened to the shrieks of kids going through the Haunted House and itched with impatience and anxiety.

Stefan paced from one side of the room to the other and hesitated in the doorway, listening carefully. The red light that illuminated the room turned his skin a ghastly shade. Things were coming to a crisis, Elena could see that. Stefan's jaw was set, and he was kneading the bridge of his nose between his finger and thumb. He was worried that Damon might be feeding on humans while he and Elena waited in the wrong place. Finally, he straightened, making up his mind, and stepped toward the entrance once more.

Just then, a hooded figure came through the door, black robes sweeping around him. The Grim Reaper regarded Stefan silently for a moment, scythe clutched in front of him, and then he swept back his hood.

"Hello, little brother," Damon said, showing his teeth in what looked more like a snarl than a smile.

Stefan looked at him gravely. "I've been waiting for you, Damon," he said.

Damon cocked a cynical eyebrow. "Saint Stefan," he said mockingly. "Does the lovely Elena want you to make peace? Stop me from making a new family?" He moved closer, resting a hand lightly on Stefan's shoulder, and Elena saw Stefan flinch. Stefan was, she realized, afraid.

When he spoke, though, his voice was steady. "It's been a long time since I thought talking to you would do any good, Damon. If you want family, I'm here. All I can do is try to stop you from doing your worst, from doing something you'll regret."

Damon's smile widened. "You stop me, baby brother? All you do is ruin everything, without even trying to." He pulled Stefan closer, his hand clamping down on Stefan's shoulder like a vise.

Moving so fast that Elena had no time to react, not even to gasp, he spun Stefan around and slammed him into the wall, sinking his teeth deep into Stefan's throat. Stefan gave a small choked moan of pain, and Elena flinched.

Damon hadn't taken care, hadn't bothered to soothe Stefan the way he would have a human. He wanted to this to hurt.

A terrible ripping noise came from the grappling brothers—Damon's teeth tearing something in Stefan's throat—and Elena clenched her fists. *This was a stupid plan*, she realized. *Damon's angry enough to kill Stefan.*

Just as she began to step forward out of her hiding place, a new voice, cool and arrogant, rang out.

"Stop it." Katherine, her head held high and her mouth thin and angry, was suddenly beside them. Damon lifted his head, his mouth dripping with blood from his brother's throat, and they both stared at her.

She was wearing the Renaissance dress Aunt Judith had made for Elena's Halloween costume, and she looked lovely, as delicate and ornate as an expensive doll, just the way she must have looked five hundred years before. The red lighting changed the ice blue of the dress to a pale violet and threw pink shadows on Katherine's pale face and golden hair.

Elena had thought that Stefan and Damon might mistake Katherine for Elena, just for a second, but it was clear that neither of them had the least doubt about who she was.

"Katherine," Stefan said. His face was full of mixed emotions. Shock, disbelief, dawning joy, and relief. Fear. "But that's impossible. It can't be. You're dead. ..."

Katherine laughed, a brittle, desperately unhappy laugh. "I wanted you to believe that. Your little human toy, the one who looks so much like me, *she* figured it out, but you never did."

"Elena?" Damon asked, his eyes narrowing suspiciously.

Katherine circled them, head held high. Her long skirts swept the floor with a quiet susurration, and Damon turned slowly, so that he was always facing her, tense and wary. "Your Elena convinced me to tell you the truth."

"Tell us then," Stefan said steadily.

"I wanted us all to be happy," Katherine said, looking back and forth between Stefan and Damon. Under the red lights, tears glistened on her cheeks. "I loved you. But it wasn't good enough for you. I wanted you to love each other, but you wouldn't. I thought if I died, you *would* love each other."

Elena had heard Katherine's story before. She let the words wash over her and concentrated on Stefan and Damon's faces as Katherine unfolded her tale: how she had another talisman against the sun made and given her maid her ring. How the maid had burned fat in the fireplace and filled Katherine's best dress with it, left it in the sun along with Katherine's note telling Stefan and Damon she couldn't bear to be the cause of strife between them. That she hoped that, once she was gone, they would come together.

Katherine's face was paler than ever, her eyes huge, tears running down her cheeks. The story had taken her back, and it was in the hurt, puzzled voice of the young girl she had been that she exclaimed, "You didn't listen, and you ran and got swords. You killed each other. *Why?* You made your deaths my fault."

Stefan's face was wet with tears, too, and he was as caught up in the memory as she was. "It was my fault, Katherine, not yours. I attacked first," he said in a choked voice. "You don't know how sorry I've been, how many times I've prayed to take it all back. I murdered my own brother. ..."

Damon was watching him intently, his eyes dark and opaque. Elena couldn't tell what he was thinking. Surely this was what he needed? To know their centuries of enmity had been pointless, that his brother regretted striking that blow and dooming them both?

Stefan turned to him. "Please, Damon," Stefan said, his voice cracking. "I'm sorry. What we've fought about for so long, hated each other over"—he gestured to Katherine—"none of it was real."

Trembling, Stefan reached a hand toward his brother, and something snapped shut in Damon's expression. He stepped away as quickly as a cat.

"Well, it's lovely to know that you've survived," he said, turning to Katherine. His voice sharpened. "But don't flatter yourself that I've spent the last five hundred years pining over you. It's not about you anymore, Katherine. It hasn't been, not for a long time."

As he spoke, his eyes fixed on the spot where Elena was hiding. *He's known I'm here all along,* she realized. She stepped out from behind the dummy. "Please, Damon," she began.

But Damon's face was a mask of fury. "You think this changes anything, Elena? I'm not going to forgive you so you can live happily ever after with my whining weakling of a baby brother. The world is *nothing* but suffering, and the fact that one girl lived when we thought she was dead doesn't make any difference. This doesn't change my plans."

Moving too quickly for their eyes to follow, Damon was gone.

## 27

"He's beautiful," Katherine said, "but he's always had that rage inside him. When he was human, I thought it was romantic."

"We have to stop him," Elena said to Stefan. "In this mood, he'll kill anyone who gets in his way."

"You promised me I would save them," Katherine said. Her face began to crumble with disappointment. "You said I'd be a hero."

There was a glimmer of violence in Katherine's eyes. Elena remembered the white tiger Katherine could become, the cruelty of the Katherine she'd met the first time she'd gone through this. Elena's lips parted. She had to say something to defuse the situation.

"I want what you wanted for us, Katherine," Stefan cut in. His face was more open than Elena had seen it in this time. "You sacrificed everything for us, and I won't forget that. But we have to find Damon before it's too late. Before your sacrifice was for nothing."

In a moment of sympathy and understanding, Katherine approached Stefan. Elena saw in Katherine what she'd been feeling for the past few weeks—loss of true love. Katherine pressed her lips to Stefan's cheek, as gently as a human would. And then in the blink of an eye, Katherine was gone.

"Come on," Elena said, gripping Stefan by the hand and pulling him out the door of the Torture Chamber. "We have to find him."

A giggling group of girls pushed past them into the Torture Chamber, and Elena hesitated in the passageway, looking both ways. The Haunted House was teeming with people. Which way would Damon have gone?

Stefan pushed her gently toward her left. "You go that way," he said grimly. "I'll work my way back toward the entrance. There are only so many places he could be."

"Check on the Druid Room first," Elena said. They needed to make sure he wasn't anywhere near Mr. Tanner. "We'll find him, Stefan."

*Of course, we don't know what we'll be able to do if we find him,* a nagging voice remarked in the back of Elena's mind. Still, she headed through the maze of rooms, her eyes raking the shadows, looking for the Grim Reaper. There were a lot of people in black-robed costumes, but none of them were Damon.

An engine revved behind her, and Elena was shoved sideways by a shrieking group as a chainsaw-wielding masked man chased them down the hall. She took a turn between two partitions and found herself suddenly alone.

"On your way to Grandma's, Little Red?" someone whispered throatily behind her.

Elena turned to see a werewolf, its mask's muzzle dripping with gruesomely realistic blood. "Matt?" she asked uncertainly.

"Didn't they tell you to stay on the path?" The werewolf's voice got a little louder as he leered at her.

*Tyler*, Elena realized with disappointment. "Have you seen Matt?" she asked, her voice flat.

"There's more than one wolf in these woods, Little Red," Tyler told her, laying a large, hairy paw on her shoulder.

Elena shrugged it off. "Look, Tyler, I really need to find Matt. Or Meredith," she added. If she knew where they were, maybe she could hide them from Damon.

Tyler scowled. "No, I don't know where they are." He leaned against her, his breath hot on her neck. "Come play with me instead, pretty girl. I'll show you the way to Grandma's house."

"If you see them—or Caroline or Bonnie—tell them I'm looking for them, okay?"

He huffed a sigh. "Whatever." Two girls Elena didn't know turned the corner into the other end of the hall, and Tyler lost interest in Elena. "Full moon, ladies," he shouted, walking toward them, and tipped his head back in a throaty howl as they giggled.

Elena passed through the Spider Room next, but there was no one there but a bunch of rowdy junior-high boys, batting the rubber spiders at each other. The Living Dead Room was teeming with people, one of whom, moaning, *"Braaaaains,"* pretended to take a bite out of Elena's face. But there was no black-clad Meredith in a witch costume, no werewolf Matt, no Egyptian Caroline.

Dread settled in the pit of Elena's stomach. Could Damon have trapped them all in the fated Druid Room? Could Stefan be outnumbered? Bonnie ought to be there too, playing a priestess sacrificing Mr. Tanner. At least she knew where Bonnie was supposed to be.

*I told her it was going to be all right,* Elena remembered. Half running, she headed for the Druid Room.

Bonnie wasn't there. There was no one poised above the altar, although Elena could hear shrieks and laughter coming from not far away. Strobe lights flashed, giving the whole room a dizzying, dreamlike quality. Beneath the cardboard Stonehenge, Mr. Tanner was stretched out across the sacrificial stone altar, his robes heavily stained with blood, his eyes blankly staring up at the ceiling. Beside him lay the ritual knife in a pool of blood.

The chill in Elena's center hardened into a frightened little ball. She rushed toward him, trying to see if Mr. Tanner was breathing. His eyes were rolled back in his head, showing little more than the whites.

She bent over the still figure, working up the nerve to touch him. "Mr. Tanner?" she said softly. *Too late, too late,* the little voice in the back of her head mourned. If Damon had managed to kill Mr. Tanner, then Elena was dead, Damon was dead, Stefan was dead.

Elena extended a shaking hand, her heart hammering, to touch Mr. Tanner's neck, to feel for a pulse.

Just before her hand made contact, Mr. Tanner sat up. "AAAAARRRGGGGGHHHH!" he shrieked into her face.

Elena screamed, a thin, high sound of shock and backpedaled away from him, banging her hip hard against the wall. Stiffly, Mr. Tanner lay back down in the same position, his eyes rolling back into his head again. A small, pleased smile tugged at the corners of his mouth.

Pressing a hand against her chest, Elena tried to calm her wildly pounding heart. She took a deep breath as it started to sink in: Mr. Tanner was still alive. She hadn't failed. She could still save herself, save them all.

lena rushed from room to room, looking for the others. She was panting, but she couldn't stop to catch her breath. She had to stop Damon before it was too late.

"Elena." Outside the Mad Slasher Room, Stefan came toward her, his dark clothes and hair blending into the shadows of the hall, only his pale face and white shirtfront standing out clearly. Elena stopped, eager for news. "I found Meredith," he said. "She's up at the front with a lot of other people, taking money."

"She should be safe there," Elena said. "As long as she doesn't head out alone." Meredith was in charge of the whole Haunted House; she could be called into the more isolated recesses of the warehouse at any moment.

Stefan glanced away, a touch of color rising in his cheeks. "I, er, Influenced her to stick with the group instead of wandering off by herself."

"Good thinking," Elena said. "Now we just need to find everyone else."

The Mad Slasher Room was packed and full of noise. A boy with a chainsaw was enthusiastically revving it, chasing screaming victims around the room. Fake blood was grotesquely sprayed across the walls, and less noisy maniacs strangled and hacked at anyone who came close. Elena jumped and shuddered as the laughing, shrieking victims shoved past her.

They were playing at blood and death, and Damon could be anywhere, watching, ready to tear them apart. She felt sick as she tried to make out individual faces and costumes in the crowd.

There was no Grim Reaper, no Egyptian priestess, no werewolf, no Druid.

In contrast, the Alien Encounter Room was quiet when they passed through. Bright beams of light flashed on and off overhead, while a girl stretched out on a table below was poked and prodded by gray alien-looking figures. The girl glanced up and winked at Elena, and Elena realized it was Sue Carson.

No one Elena and Stefan were looking for.

Caroline should have been in the Deaths from History Room, playing with a rubber snake, but she wasn't.

Turning to leave, Elena caught sight of red curls peeking out from under the black hood of a rather short executioner wielding a plastic axe over Anne Boleyn's head. Grabbing hold of the executioner's axe arm, she asked, "Bonnie? What are you doing here?"

"Ray had to go to the bathroom," Bonnie explained, pulling off the hood. Underneath, she looked a little sweaty and disheveled, strands of hair sticking to her forehead. "I said I'd take over for a few minutes."

"Bonnie, Damon's here somewhere," Elena said. "Have you seen Matt or Caroline?"

Bonnie sobered. "Caroline ought to be here," she said. "Everyone's been wondering where she is. The last time I saw Matt was in the Fun House. I'll come with you." She propped the plastic axe against the wall and led the way, Stefan and Elena hurrying after her.

The entrance to the Fun House was concealed behind a long black curtain. As Elena reached to twitch it aside, a hooded figure stepped out, black clothes swirling all around it. Elena jerked backward, her breath catching in her throat.

But the dark figure was too short to be Damon.

"Vickie?" Elena said, peering beneath the hood. "Have you seen Matt or Caroline?"

Vickie frowned, thinking hard. "I can't say," she said.

Beside her, Elena felt Stefan stiffen, turning his full focus onto Vickie. "You can't say?" he asked slowly. "Vickie, can we come into the Fun House?"

"The Fun House is closed," Vickie told them.

"What? No, it's not," Bonnie said, and tried to dodge past her, but Vickie shoved her backward.

"You can't go in there," she said. There was something flat behind Vickie's usually timid brown eyes, and Elena finally figured out what was going on: Damon had compelled Vickie to keep them out.

Stefan wouldn't be able to compel Vickie to let them in—his Power wasn't as strong as Damon's—but he was stronger than any human. Her eyes met Stefan's green ones, and she knew they were in perfect agreement. He would have to overpower Vickie.

"Hang on," Bonnie said. Her small hand gripped Elena's, and she pulled on Stefan's arm with her other hand. She tugged them down the hall with her, looking back to smile over her shoulder at Vickie.

"Damon's compelled her," Stefan said, pulling out of Bonnie's grasp as soon as they turned the corner away from Vickie's gaze. "Caroline or Matt—maybe both of them— must be in the Fun House. There isn't much time."

"I know," Bonnie said. "But there's another way into the Fun House."

Crooking a finger for Elena and Stefan to follow, Bonnie led them to a narrow opening between two partitions and pulled aside a swathe of black cloth. "Duck under here," she said softly, "and we'll come out on the other end of the Fun House."

"You're the best, Bonnie," Elena whispered and ducked under the cloth.

When Elena straightened up, she had to blink and shield her eyes for a moment. Strobe lights were flashing here, too, but far faster and brighter than in the Druid Room, as if they had been turned up to their maximum settings.

In one bright flash of light, Elena saw a twisted face, pale and staring. A corpse. They were too late, she realized, with numb horror. Everything was lost.

"Elena?" Stefan asked. He must have been able to hear the panicked change in her breathing. The lights flashed again and she realized there was no corpse, just her own reflection, distorted by a fun-house mirror.

The mirrors were everywhere. An image of Elena and Bonnie stretched out like rubber bands stood by a reflection of Stefan with an enormous head. Loud carnival music blared all around them.

The whole effect was dizzying, and Elena wanted to shut her eyes, but there was no time. They had to find Damon.

The hall of mirrors curved in front of them, and they couldn't see the other end. Cocking her head to indicate the direction, Elena led Bonnie and Stefan up the hall, stumbling as the lights dimmed, then flashed again.

As they rounded the bend, she saw Damon and Caroline, reflected over and over. There were a hundred Damon and Carolines in the flashes of light, all around her, squashed and bulbous, long and thin, bulging oddly.

In the center, two perfectly beautiful people, one human and one vampire, were locked in what was almost an embrace.

Damon had thrown off his cloak and wore jeans and a black button-down. His head was bent back, exposing his long white throat to Caroline. In one hand, he clasped a dagger loosely—Stefan's dagger, Elena realized, one of his stolen treasures—and Elena could see that he had made a cut along his breastbone for Caroline to feed from. Her face was pressed against Damon's chest, and, with a shudder of disgust, Elena realized Caroline was swallowing his blood eagerly.

When Caroline raised her head for a moment, her mouth was red and slick with blood. It dripped down her chin and marked her pure white shift. Elena recoiled. The girl's cat-green eyes seemed dazed, and, as she gazed up at Damon adoringly, Elena was quite sure he'd put Caroline heavily under his Power.

"Stay back, Elena," Stefan said softly.

At the sound of Stefan's voice, Damon looked up and threw him a dazzling, brief smile. Turning Caroline gently around so that she faced them, he raised his dagger and laid it against her throat. Caroline hung in his grasp, blinking slowly, not seeming to even see them.

"No," Stefan said. Elena could feel him tensing himself for one desperate run at Damon. And she knew, as surely as if she had seen it, that if Stefan made a move toward him, Damon would cut Caroline's throat.

"Stop," she said, her voice breaking. "Everybody, just stop." She pushed back her own red hood so that she and Damon could see each other more clearly. His eyes held hers, wide and dark, and his lips tipped up in a mocking smile.

"You *need* each other, you and Stefan," she said. "Why are you trying to make another family when your family is here?"

Damon sneered. "Family. Stefan hasn't been my family since he stuck a sword through my heart."

Beside her, Elena felt Stefan stiffen. Then he stepped forward. "There is *nothing* I regret more than that. I killed you. My only brother." His green eyes were full of tears. "Even if I lived forever, I could never make it up to you."

Damon stared at him, his handsome face blank.

"Remember how Stefan followed you when you were a child?" Elena asked. "He'd take a beating from your father rather than ever betray your secrets. He *worshipped* you." She felt Stefan glance at her curiously, wondering how Elena could know that, but it didn't matter now. She kept her attention firmly fixed on Damon.

Was his grip on the dagger pressed to Caroline's throat loosening? Elena wasn't sure.

"Remember Incognita, the beautiful black mare you won playing cards, when you were just sixteen?" Stefan said hoarsely. "That morning when you brought her home, you let me ride behind you, and we went so fast, her hooves hardly touched the ground. We were invincible then. Happy."

Surely the taut line of Damon's mouth was softening, Elena thought. The dagger had slipped a little, resting gently against Caroline's throat as she sagged, half-conscious in Damon's arms. But then Damon tensed again.

"Sentimental tales from the nursery," he scoffed. "Those children have been dead for centuries." He took a fresh grip on the knife.

"It still matters," Elena said desperately. "You're both still *here*. There are only two people left in the world who remember you when you were alive, Damon. Once Stefan is gone, only Katherine will remember, and she's the one who changed you. No one else knows anything but the monster. It's not too late to change that."

Damon hesitated for a split second. "Again with these promises you can't keep. If you want the good brother, you already have him."

Elena shook her head. "No," she said. "This isn't about that. I never had either of you, not in this world."

Damon's forehead creased in a puzzled frown, but Stefan held out his hands to his brother beseechingly, walking slowly toward him. "I never meant to kill you," he said, as softly and soothingly as he would have spoken to a wild animal. "I would spend the rest of my days trying to right that wrong, if you would be my brother again."

There was a long, tense moment. The cheerful, hectic carnival music was at odds with the mood of the room.

In a quick motion, Damon pushed Caroline forward so that she fell onto the floor, landing hard and lying motionless. Bonnie gasped and rushed to her.

Looking past Stefan, Damon's black eyes met Elena's. "I won't turn your friends," he said shortly. His gaze shifted back to Stefan's. "I won't kill you, either, I suppose. Not now at least."

There was no embrace between Stefan and Damon, no show of catharsis. But Elena caught a hint of a smile on Damon's face—a small, private smile Elena had seen before, in the future she left behind. It was a smile Damon only ever gave to his brother.

Joy flooded through her, as if she was filling with sunlight. Mr. Tanner had survived. Bonnie and Meredith and Matt and Caroline—who Bonnie was fussing over now—were still human. Halloween night was almost over.

She was going to have a future. They were all going to live.

## 29

"**I**t went really well, don't you think?" Meredith said, tucking a long lock of dark hair behind her ear and looking up at the closed entrance to the Haunted House.

It was late, but they'd only managed to clear out all the customers about half an hour before. Across the parking lot, the last of the costumed workers were climbing into their cars, laughing and calling good-byes to one another. The heavy clouds that had hung overhead at the beginning of the evening had cleared and now stars shone brightly in the sky.

Elena linked her arms through Bonnie and Meredith's, pulling her best friends close, and smiled at Matt beside them. "I thought it was amazing."

Stefan and Damon had disappeared somewhere together shortly after their reconciliation, but that was all right with Elena. She was happy, for now, to have this last time with her oldest, dearest friends.

And it *was* the last time, she was suddenly sure of it. The Guardians hadn't sent Elena to start over; they had only sent her to change things. There would probably be an Elena here tomorrow, she thought, but she was pretty sure it wouldn't be her, it wouldn't be the Elena who had lived this more than once.

She was going to wake up in that Elena's future, whatever future she had made. And she hoped that Matt, Meredith, and Bonnie would be part of that future somehow, but they wouldn't be the ones she knew now.

This was good-bye.

"You did such a good job planning the whole thing, Meredith," Elena said. "It seems like you can do anything you put your mind to. You're *wonderful*."

Meredith's olive cheeks flushed pink. "Thanks," she said, dipping her head shyly.

They'd reached Matt's car, and Meredith opened the passenger door and climbed in. As Matt crossed to the driver's side, Elena hugged him. "You're one of the best people I know, you know that?" she said. She was choking up a little. "I *promise* everything will be okay. Remember that."

Kissing her on the cheek, Matt drew back with a little rueful half smile. "You still have to help us clean up the Haunted House tomorrow," he told her. Elena just laughed.

As Matt closed the car door behind him, Elena turned to see Bonnie watching her with an affectionate, knowing gaze. "This is it, huh?" she said. She was smiling, but her lips were quivering a little.

"I guess so," Elena told her.

With a sniff, Bonnie threw herself into Elena's arms and held her tightly.

"Oh, Scarecrow," Elena murmured into her friend's bright curls. "I think I'll miss you most of all."

After one tight hug, Bonnie pulled back, swiping a hand quickly under her eyes. "Seven years in the future isn't that long. You'll see me then."

"I hope so," Elena said. She reached out and took Bonnie's hand for a moment, squeezing it tightly. She tried to memorize the feeling of Bonnie's small, strong hand gripping hers.

She would remember this, just in case. She would remember Matt's open, honest face, and Meredith's wry smile. Whatever happened, she wouldn't forget them.

For now, there was one more thing she had to tell Bonnie. "You should go talk to Mrs. Flowers. You saw how much Power you have, and she'll be able to teach you how to use it. I expect you to be crazy-powerful seven years from now."

"Aye aye, Captain," Bonnie said, saluting ridiculously. Then her gaze slipped past Elena and Elena turned to follow it.

Stefan was crossing the parking lot toward them. Elena and Bonnie exchanged a glance.

"I'll tell the others to wait. Take your time," Bonnie said, and slipped into the car.

Elena walked slowly toward Stefan. As she reached him, he looked down into Elena's eyes. There were no words worthy of expressing what either of them felt.

Elena wanted to take him in her arms and hold on tight, but she didn't. He wasn't hers now.

She might never see him again. The thought filled her with an almost painful sorrow, but not with the angry bewilderment she'd felt at his death. Now she had the chance to say good-bye.

Stefan's green eyes searched hers, as if he was looking for answers. "I wanted to say thank you," he said finally. "Damon and I are leaving. We've decided to go back to Italy for now. I wanted—*we* wanted—to see what's left of the Florence we remember." His lips quirked up in a half smile. "We'll see if we can find more of our humanity there, I suppose."

Elena nodded. "I'm glad," she said.

He reached out and took her hands, so gently and carefully that Elena's heart ached with longing. "What can I do to thank you?" he said slowly.

Elena squeezed his hand once, fiercely, and then pulled away. "You don't need to thank me," she said, hearing the roughness of almost-tears in her own voice. "Just take care of Damon. And of yourself."

She turned toward the car where her friends were waiting, and Stefan touched her on the shoulder. "Will I see you again?" he asked.

"I don't know," she said honestly. "I don't think so. But just ... keep going, okay? For yourself, and for Damon. Remember that there's someone out there who cares about you, the real you."

"You are a mysterious one, Elena Gilbert," Stefan said. With one last nod of appreciation, Stefan turned to go.

Hot tears were running down her cheeks as Elena watched Stefan walk out of her life forever. But Elena wasn't sad, or not only sad. This Stefan might live. And that made it all worthwhile.

s Elena rode home in the backseat of Matt's car, her thoughts drifted to the one person she hadn't gotten a chance to say good-bye to. Maybe it was for the best. She didn't know how she'd say good-bye to Damon.

In the front seat, Matt and Meredith were laughing, talking about the Haunted House. They'd missed *everything*. With luck, they'd never know about vampires, never be touched by the darkness all around them. They'd be normal. Happy.

Bonnie jostled Elena gently. "Are you okay?" she whispered.

Elena sighed and laid her head on her friend's shoulder, just for a moment.

Bonnie wrapped an arm around her shoulders. "You helped them. From what you told me, I think you've saved a lot of people."

"Yeah," Elena said, her voice small. She blinked back the sting of tears in her eyes. She'd saved herself, too. Stefan. Damon.

In the big picture, it didn't matter if she never got to say good-bye to Damon, if she never saw either Salvatore brother again. Not if they all got to live.

When they pulled up to her house, Elena hugged all three of her friends again, fast and hard, before climbing out of the car and waving good-bye.

Aunt Judith had left the porch light on for her, but the windows of the house were dark. They must already be in bed.

As Elena crossed the lawn, a dark shape detached itself from the shadows beneath the quince tree and came toward her.

"Damon," she said, happiness flaring up inside her, hot and sudden.

Damon came close and looked at Elena for a few moments without speaking, his black eyes unreadable. "I suppose I should say thank you," he said at last.

"You're welcome," Elena said, holding his gaze steadily.

"You're no coward," Damon gave her his quick, devastating smile.

Elena smiled back, and Damon took her by the arm and led her to her front porch. "More comfortable here," he said, sitting down on the porch steps, and Elena sat beside him. She was still wearing the Red Riding Hood cloak, and she was glad of its warmth.

Damon tilted his head back to look at the stars. "I suppose Stefan told you we've decided to go back to Italy," he said conversationally. "He seems to think that things might get sticky here, with the fire and the graveyard desecration and all that." Damon lifted one shoulder in a graceful shrug.

"I can imagine," Elena said. She let herself lean into him a little bit. She felt as if her heart was, very quietly, breaking.

"Come with us," Damon said suddenly. "I have this strange feeling that it would be a terrible mistake to leave you behind."

He was still looking up at the stars, as intensely as if he could read the future written in the sky. The moonlight and the porch light combined threw shadows across his face, softening Damon's aristocratic features and the stubborn set of his mouth.

"Oh, Damon," Elena said. Tears started to pool in her eyes.

Damon tore his gaze away from the sky and looked at her, his eyes dark and more open than she had ever seen them in this time. "Come," he said again. "Please."

"I can't," Elena said. Damon flinched and, on an impulse, she put out one hand and covered his heart.

"You're good," she told him furiously. "In here. You can be so good, so *wonderful* if you decide to be. Don't forget that."

Tears ran down Elena's face, hot on her cold skin. She scrambled to her feet and backed away toward the front door.

"Good-bye, Damon," she said quickly, longingly. His face was full of confusion, and he started to rise, but she was already closing the door behind her.

Elena leaned against the door and just let the tears fall. Every part of her yearned to go with Stefan and Damon.

What if she did? Would she wake up in a future where she and Damon and Stefan had been traveling Europe together, a happy triumvirate, for the last seven years?

*No.* Elena shook her head. She wasn't going to be selfish like that, not the way she'd always been selfish with the Salvatore brothers. She'd seen where it led. She wasn't going to make Katherine's mistakes. Not again.

Wiping her eyes, Elena peered out the window by the front door, but Damon was gone.

Her shoulders slumped and Elena started up the stairs, feeling unutterably exhausted.

Margaret's trick-or-treat bag was in the hall outside her door, stuffed with candy, and Elena smiled a little.

Turning into her own bedroom, Elena kicked off her shoes and lay down on the bed, not bothering to change into her nightgown.

A tear slipped out from under her eyelids and ran slowly down her cheek. But a certain peace settled over Elena, and as she fell into a slumber, she knew without a doubt that, as much as it hurt, she'd done the right thing.

## 31

Elena woke up in a room flooded with light. The white ceiling above her was unfamiliar, outlined with ornate crown molding. Sitting up, she looked around. She was in a big bed heaped with soft pillows and a thick duvet. Sunlight streamed in through full-length windows at one end of the room, which opened onto a tiny balcony she could just see from the bed.

Hopping out of bed, Elena wiggled her toes against the thick pale carpet and padded out barefoot to examine the rest of the apartment. She wasn't in the clothes she'd fallen asleep in anymore, she realized, but in crisp white cotton pajamas. Elena ran a hand across them wonderingly.

It wasn't a big apartment: bedroom, bathroom, a kitchen with a small dining alcove at one end, a little living room with a large, cushy pale green couch. Everything looked peaceful and comfortable in light, neutral shades, accented with forest green or jewel blue. Paintings hung on the walls—not posters, but real paintings, a couple of them abstract, one an intricate landscape, another a charcoal sketch of a young girl's face. The apartment felt like a nest, a retreat made just for one. Just for her.

It felt like home, she realized, even though she'd never seen it before.

She rummaged through the kitchen, finding coffee and figuring out the intimidatingly complicated brushed-steel coffee maker. While it brewed, she went back into the bedroom to get dressed. Everything in the closet seemed simple and chic, more sophisticated than the old Elena had been used to, and she pulled on a pair of close-fitting black trousers and a light blue top made of impossibly soft fabric.

Picking up a hairbrush, she looked into the mirror and froze. For a moment, she held her breath, examining the almost-stranger in the mirror.

She looked *older*. Not too old, but like she was in her mid-twenties. Her hair was shorter, falling just past her chin, and there were a few tiny lines beginning at the corners of her eyes, as if she'd been squinting in the sun. Elena tilted her head, watching the swing of her hair against her cheek. She looked good, she thought.

In the life she'd lived with Stefan, Elena had drunk the Waters of Eternal Life and Youth at age eighteen, and stopped getting older. Stopped changing. She hadn't wanted to age while Stefan stayed young, had wanted to be by his side for eternity.

It had been the right choice when they had been together. After Stefan had been killed, it had seemed like living death to go on without him forever, to never grow old or have the possibility of having children. Now she would get to *change*. She had grown up, and she would keep aging.

As she turned away from the mirror, Elena's gaze fell upon something on her bedside table that she hadn't seen before: a golden ball, just the right size to fit comfortably in her palm. Picking it up, Elena pressed the catch and watched the ball unfold into a small golden hummingbird set with gems.

The music box Damon had given her.

Was it possible? Had they found each other again, somewhere in the intervening years between Fell's Church and now? Her heart began to pound wildly, full of hope.

Carefully, she put the music box back on the table. There was a crisply folded note next to where it had stood. Elena picked the note up with shaking hands and unfolded it.

> *Well done, Elena. Here is a small souvenir of your past life, as a token of our regard. Enjoy your humanity—you've earned it. I hope you find your true destiny. Mylea*

The Celestial Guardians had given her a piece of the life she had lost. It was a kind gesture, she knew, but it pierced a whole in her heart. A token could never replace the love she had sacrificed. No home could be home without someone to share it with.

Stepping out onto the balcony, Elena gazed over the city before her, and felt her mouth drop open. Far away, over the rooftops, she could just glimpse the Eiffel Tower.

"Hideous," she suddenly remembered Damon saying, that last day together in Paris. "A truly tragic streetlamp."

Elena stifled a giggle. *She* thought it was beautiful, anyway.

Wow. She lived in *Paris*.

Energized, Elena turned to the task of figuring out just who Elena Gilbert was in this new future. She rifled through her drawers, read her own papers, sorted through the mail. Rummaging through the cupboards and refrigerator, she devoured the chewy bread, soft cheese, and crisp fruit she found inside.

By the time a couple of hours had passed, she knew that she worked at an art gallery. She had an undergraduate degree in art history, from the Université de Paris. Apparently, Elena had come to Paris for a junior year abroad from the University of Virginia—not Dalcrest College—and never left, finishing her education here.

She had lived alone in this apartment for two years, according to her lease. There were notes from friends in both English and French—and it was a relief to realize that she could read French much more fluently than she had been able to in her old life. Elena smiled over a gossipy birthday card from Aunt Judith that made it clear that she and Robert and Margaret were just as happy in this life as in Elena's previous one.

There was no sign of any romance. Elena's heart ached a little at that. But who could she have loved after the Salvatore brothers?

Just as Elena was sweeping papers back into her desk drawers, there was a tapping at her front door.

Leaping up, Elena rushed toward it. It was Bonnie, she was sure of it, or Meredith. She could picture them here. Meredith probably had helped Elena pick out the chic outfits. Bonnie must have cast a protection spell over the whole apartment.

She flung open the door.

"Elena!" said the dark-haired girl on the other side, her arms full of shopping bags. Elena had never seen her before. She kissed Elena enthusiastically on each cheek in greeting. "Can I leave these here? Come on, we'll be late."

She said it all in French, very fast, and Elena was relieved to realize she spoke and understood French as well as she read it.

A name popped into Elena's head, along with a remembered warm affection. "Veronique," she greeted her friend. "Where are we going?"

Veronique made a little moue of pretended offense. "You forgot our Sunday lunch?" she asked. "The others are probably already there."

The restaurant at which they had lunch was as stylish and tasteful as the rest of Elena's new life. The two friends waiting for them there were as lovely as Veronique was. They jumped to their feet and kissed Veronique and Elena on both cheeks, laughing. Elena laughed with them, knowing beyond a shadow of a doubt that these were people she loved.

She just wished she could remember them properly.

After a few minutes she got them all straight. Veronique was talkative and bossy, with a quick, good-humored smile. She was a stockbroker, and she and Elena had been roommates in college. Elena had a flash of memory: Veronique, softer and younger, her hair tied up in a sloppy bun, hollow-eyed from staying up late studying for exams.

Lina was quieter and more soft-spoken, with huge dreamy eyes and long light-brown hair. She worked at the gallery with Elena and was the niece of the owner.

And Manon, sharp-witted and sarcastic with very short, very pale blonde hair, was a graduate student at the

Sorbonne, doing a joint degree in art history and law. She had gone to university with Elena and Veronique.

"If you want to get further with art history," she was advising Elena, "you should come back to school. The museums will never hire someone with only an undergraduate degree."

"Perhaps," Elena said, sipping her wine. She hadn't found school particularly interesting back in the life she remembered. There had been too much else to do: monsters to fight, the ongoing drama of her love life to manage.

Maybe here, studying something she loved, with the idea that it would actually help her get a particular job ... She felt excitement blossom in her chest. She could tell from the way Manon was talking that the Elena these girls knew was serious about her career.

Lina began to describe a show she and Elena were organizing at the gallery to the other girls, and Elena listened, eyes wide.

"It was Elena who suggested arranging the pieces by the models instead of chronologically," Lina said. "A very interesting effect. He used the same models over and over, for years, and you can see the women growing older, just as his art developed."

Elena felt a flush of pride. Even though she didn't remember it, apparently she was good at her job.

"Let's talk about something more interesting than art," Veronique said eventually. "Elena. Are you going to go out with Hugo again?"

*Hugo?* Elena tried to prompt the memory that had given her the names of her friends, but came up blank. "I don't know," she said slowly.

In unison, all three girls sighed.

"He's such a nice man," Lina said, tucking a long lock of hair behind her ear. "And he's crazy about you."

"I will take him off your hands if you don't want him," Manon said. "That lovely man, just going to waste." She rolled her eyes exaggeratedly, laughing.

"Obviously, you shouldn't date anyone you don't want," Veronique added, "but it seems like you're never even open to the *idea* of love."

Elena didn't know what to say. Even without memories of this time, she knew why she wasn't looking for love, why she wasn't falling for the lovely man they were talking about. How could she? She had left her heart with Damon and Stefan, wherever they were. Finally, she shrugged. "Sometimes it's not meant to be, I guess."

"We worry about you," Veronique said flatly. "It's like you're waiting for something, and we don't want you to let life pass you by."

Looking back at her Parisian friends, Elena was hit by a sudden rush of homesickness. Meredith and Bonnie would have fussed over her and nudged her in just the same way. Where were they now? Had the vow they had sworn in the churchyard, to be friends forever, come true? *I hope so,* she thought. *I hope I haven't lost everyone from my old life, even if I've lost … even if I can't have …*

"Oh, we didn't mean to make you sad," Lina said softly, laying a warm soft hand over hers. "It will all come right in the end."

* * *

When she came back from lunch, the apartment seemed entirely too quiet. Elena wandered through the flat, touching the sleek pale furniture, rearranging the books and ornaments.

It was exactly the kind of place she'd always dreamed of. And yet, she felt terribly wistful.

She was reminding herself of Damon, she realized. How he had brushed his fingers across her possessions, opened drawers to peer inside, inspected her photographs. Like him, she was trying to figure out the person who lived here.

Elena laughed a little and wiped her eyes. The person who lived here had a wonderful life. Elena just wasn't sure if it was really hers.

In the kitchen, she found an invitation held by a magnet to the refrigerator, something she'd somehow managed to overlook on her first rummage through the apartment.

Elena read: ". . . invite you to the wedding of their daughter Bonnie Mae McCullough to Zander—" She stopped.

*Zander?* She could feel a smile beginning on her face.

Some things must be destined after all.

*mazing.* Despite everything that had changed, Bonnie was not only marrying the same guy, she'd chosen the same bridesmaids' dresses. As she waited to walk down the aisle behind Bonnie's two older sisters, Elena carefully straightened the long rose pink gown and held her bouquet—pale lilies and bright roses—at waist level.

This time, though, the wedding was in the church Bonnie's parents attended, and there seemed to be a lot more people in attendance. Elena looked over the crowd, picking out faces she recognized: Sue Carson, Bonnie's dad's business partner, Mrs. Flowers. Apparently, when Bonnie's mom and sisters had time to get involved, things got a lot more elaborate.

Someone struck up the wedding march, and the bridesmaids began to file in, first Bonnie's sisters; then Shay,

Zander's second-in-command in the Pack; then a girl Elena didn't know who had been Bonnie's roommate at Dalcrest College; then Meredith, head held high, stepped down the aisle.

Meredith looked terrific. Confident and elegant, her beautiful thick dark hair piled on top of her head. And she was *human*. Elena let the spreading joy of that fact run through her. The changes Elena had made back during those fateful few months in high school had saved Meredith.

When it was Elena's turn, she raised her head high, held her flowers low, and stepped carefully and slowly, just the way she'd been told. At the front of the church, she took her place next to Meredith and looked over at the guys' side of the aisle.

It was all werewolves—Matt and Zander must not be good friends here—jostling one another rowdily, but they stilled and came to attention as Zander lifted his head, pushing his pale blond hair out of his eyes, and saw Bonnie.

She looked beautiful. She came down the aisle on her father's arm, draped in creamy lace. Pink rosebuds were twined in her hair. Bonnie and Zander gazed at each other, and they both looked so incredibly happy that Elena's breath caught in her throat.

"Dearly beloved," the minister said, and Elena listened with only half an ear as she watched Bonnie and Zander take each other's hands and smile at each other, a warm, private smile.

Elena had gotten a chance to talk to Bonnie last night after the rehearsal dinner. She and Meredith and Bonnie had sat up half the night in Bonnie's room, talking things over, just like old times. When Meredith had stepped out for a minute, Elena had turned to Bonnie and breathed, "Bonnie, the last thing I remember before two weeks ago was Halloween night in Fell's Church."

Bonnie had squealed and leaped up to hug Elena. It was such a relief to have just one person to share this huge secret with, Elena thought, watching as Bonnie began to speak her vows, promising to have and to hold.

Things hadn't changed that much for Bonnie in this life. She was a witch, she had gone to Dalcrest, she taught kindergarten, she loved Zander, she lived in Colorado. She was happy. Perhaps a little softer and gentler than the Bonnie Elena had known in the future she'd left behind. This Bonnie hadn't been through so much, hadn't seen her friends die.

Meredith, on the other hand, had changed. Elena cast a sideways glance at her gray-eyed friend. Meredith was so much happier here. She didn't know anything about the supernatural, Bonnie had quietly confirmed. Well, she knew Bonnie said she was psychic, and was sort of New Agey with candles and herbs, but Meredith thought it was all a game. It was, Bonnie and Elena agreed, better that way.

Meredith had graduated from Harvard Law School. She was going to take the bar next month, and she wanted to work for the public defender's office in Boston. She wasn't a hunter. She wasn't a vampire.

Last night, when they'd been sharing gossip and updating one another on their lives, Meredith, eyes shining, had told them about the work she'd done with some of her classmates and professors, researching the cases of prisoners on death row that hadn't been handled properly, trying to prove the innocence of people who had been wrongly convicted.

"You're saving people," Elena had said, impressed. "Like a warrior." Meredith had blushed with pleasure. It didn't matter if she hunted monsters or not, Elena realized. Meredith was always going to find a way to be a hero.

"You may kiss the bride," the minister said, and Bonnie leaned up as Zander leaned down and they wrapped their arms around each other and kissed, tenderly.

Unexpectedly, tears welled up in Elena's eyes and she bit her lip, hard, to force them away.

She was so happy for Bonnie, she told herself fiercely. And her own life was wonderful, everything she would have dreamed of in a world where she didn't have to hunt monsters, didn't have to be a Guardian.

It was just that, the last time she'd been in Bonnie's wedding, she'd felt the brush of Damon's admiring regard from his seat in the audience.

Bonnie and Zander were heading down the aisle, leaving the church, and it was time to follow them. Elena took the arm of her werewolf groomsman—Spencer, the preppy one—and laughed politely at his joke without really hearing it.

Outside, it was early evening, and the leaves were just beginning to change. There was a briskness in the air, the beginning of fall. Fall, again. The last time she'd been in Fell's Church in the fall was seven years ago, although it only felt like a few weeks, the night she'd said good-bye to Stefan and Damon.

They were out there somewhere—probably—and she should be glad of it, *was* glad of it, fiercely glad that they were still alive.

She felt that wistfulness again, stronger still, at the beginning of the reception, when Jared, Zander's best man, started his toast.

"Uh ..." the shaggy-haired werewolf began, "when Zander started dating Bonnie, we all thought she was awesome, but we were like, 'Really?' because she wasn't, uh, the same kind of person we were." Looking around the circle of faces smiling at him, Jared's eyes went wide and panicky.

This was the same toast Jared had given in that other world, so Elena knew he'd be able to pull it together. But that time, Damon's eyes had met Elena's, and she had felt Damon's rich amusement coming straight through the bond between them. They'd both laughed at the same time, quiet laughter at an inside joke.

At this wedding without that bond, without Damon, Elena felt slightly adrift.

After the toast, she and Meredith picked up their place cards and found their tables at the reception. There was someone already sitting there, and Elena grinned with delight. "Matt!"

Matt—bigger and broader than the last time she'd seen him, but with the same open, friendly face—got to his feet and hugged them both. Beside him, a tiny woman, almost as tiny as Bonnie, jumped to her feet and hugged them, too, blond curls bouncing over her shoulders.

"This is Jeannette," Matt said proudly.

"I've heard so much about you!" she said, excitedly to Elena. "Matt and I keep saying we're going to come to Europe and see everything you've been e-mailing him about since college. The gallery and all."

Sue Carson and her husband and a couple of Bonnie's college friends came to join them at the table, and the next few minutes were full of greetings and introductions.

"I'm going to get another drink," Jeannette said brightly after a few minutes, hopping up from the table. "I know you want a beer, honey, and can I get anyone else anything?"

Matt watched her walk away with a fond, proud smile. "She's great, isn't she?" he asked. "Did I tell you she's finishing up vet school? And not just poodles and things. She's going to be a large animal vet. As little as she is, she can handle a bull or a wild horse."

"She seems terrific," Elena said, sipping her wine. She was happy for Matt, but she couldn't help missing Jasmine, the girlfriend he'd had for so long in the world she remembered. Maybe not everyone had a soul mate.

A thick band across one of Matt's fingers caught her eye, and she leaned forward suddenly, shocked. "Matt Honeycutt! Is that a *Super Bowl* ring?"

Matt blushed, and Meredith stared at her in disbelief. "Honestly, Elena," Meredith said. "I know you live in France, but don't you even hear who wins the Super Bowl?"

Elena was momentarily dumbfounded, but Matt just rubbed at the back of his neck, embarrassed. "It's not a big deal," he said. "I'm not first string, I only played for a little while."

"Are you kidding?" Elena said, and got up to hug him. "It's a huge deal." She held onto him tightly for a moment.

He was happy and successful. Even without Jasmine. *Maybe this is his true destiny.*

Time passed and Elena drank wine and talked to familiar faces. Dinner was served, salmon or steak, and the DJ began to play. Bonnie and Zander came out onto the dance floor for their first dance, gazing up into each other's eyes. Elena was watching their dance from the half-empty table when she looked up and saw a familiar face. *Alaric.*

He was listening to Meredith, his sandy head inclined politely as she talked, a smile on his handsome, boyish face.

Alaric Saltzman had been called in by some of the citizens of Fell's Church to investigate Mr. Tanner's death. He had taken over as their history teacher to investigate the possibility of vampires being behind Tanner's murder.

In a world where Mr. Tanner had lived, Alaric had never come to Fell's Church. They had never met him.

So why was he at Bonnie's wedding? Why was he talking to Meredith?

"Who's that with Meredith?" she asked, leaning across the table toward Matt and interrupting his conversation with Sue Carson. They both looked.

"I don't know," Matt said, and Sue shook her head. "One of Zander's friends, probably."

As they watched, Meredith took Alaric's hand and pulled him out onto the dance floor.

"He's cute," Sue said. "They look good together."

"Excuse me," Elena said, pushing back her chair and getting up.

When she found Bonnie flitting about happily between tables, the redheaded girl hugged her enthusiastically. "Was that not the best wedding?" she asked.

Zander's smile widened. "She's been saying that to everyone," he said affectionately. "I totally agree, of course, but I might be biased."

"It was a wonderful wedding," Elena agreed, "but actually I wanted to ask you, how do you know Alaric Saltzman?" On the dance floor, Alaric said something softly in Meredith's ear, and she tossed her head back and laughed.

"Alaric? Oh, the High Wolf Council called him in to consult on some problem they had a while ago," Bonnie said vaguely. "He and Zander got to be friends."

Zander added, "He's a really good guy. Meredith's okay with him."

"How do *you* know Alaric Saltzman?" Bonnie asked curiously.

"Oh." Elena shifted uncomfortably. It was way too much to explain, especially in a crowded reception hall. "It's complicated. I'm sure he won't know who I am."

"Huh. *Oh*," Bonnie said, getting it. "One of those kind of friends. Out of the past. Or a different time, anyway."

Zander frowned, looking slightly bemused, but he didn't say anything.

"Yes," Elena said. "Exactly."

A few minutes later, the photographer came over to ask Bonnie and Zander to pose with a table of Bonnie's cousins, and Elena went back to her own table. From across the room, Elena watched as Alaric and Meredith danced, and then got a drink at the bar together, laughing and leaning toward each other, Meredith reaching up unconsciously to push twirl a falling tendril of her own hair around her finger as she smiled up at him. When they went out on the dance floor again, Alaric was holding Meredith's hand firmly in his.

Elena took another sip of wine, but it suddenly tasted bitter.

She was happy for her friends. She truly was. They deserved every happiness, both of them, and Zander and Alaric were perfect partners.

But, despite that, Elena felt like the walls she'd built up inside herself were breaking, cracking, letting a flood of misery spill through her, one small stream at a time. She put down her wine glass and clenched her hands together, willing back the tears. She wasn't going to make a scene at Bonnie's wedding.

But she would grow old and die, and she would never know what had happened to Damon and Stefan. If they'd stuck together.

She might love each of them. Did love them, had a thousand memories of love, but they were only hers. They wouldn't remember.

A lump was rising up in her throat, and she knew with sudden, devastating certainty that she was about to cry after all.

"Hey," Matt said, leaning toward her. "Elena. Are you okay?"

"Of course," Elena said, her voice brittle and cracking. "I always cry at weddings."

"Sure," Matt said. "Come dance with me, then. You don't mind, do you, Jeannette?"

"Of course not," Jeannette said lightly, looking at Elena with sympathetic, intelligent eyes. "I'm going to see if I can track down a waiter to bring me more of those tiny crab cakes."

His big hand securely holding hers, Matt led Elena to a distant corner of the dance floor and wrapped his arms around her. Elena pressed her face against his shoulder, glad of the warm, reassuring bulk of him.

"Do you want to talk about it?" Matt asked softly, and Elena shook her head, not looking up.

Matt held onto Elena tightly, and she let the tears flow, her face buried in his shoulder where no one could see.

*At least I still have this,* she thought, sniffling. *At least I still have my friends.*

## 33

*Dear Diary,*

*The last four days in Virginia were wonderful ones. I went up and stayed with Aunt Judith and Robert in Richmond and spent some time with my baby sister. It's so hard to believe that Margaret's in middle school now. When I think about her, I still imagine that four-year-old with the big blue eyes, but she hasn't been that little girl for a long time. We went with Aunt Judith and got our nails done together, and Meggie even told me about a boy she likes! How can she have grown up so fast?*

Elena glanced up from her diary and out the tiny, rounded window as the wheels of her plane jolted as they landed on the runway. The sky at Charles de Gaulle airport was gray and drizzly, and just suited her mood. Elena sighed drearily and turned back to the diary.

> *I was thinking about moving back to Virginia. I'd get to see my baby sister grow up. Aunt Judith would be happy, and even Robert would be pleased.*
>
> *I've got a life in Paris, of course. Friends. A job I love.*
>
> *And none of it feels like mine.*

The plane was taxiing to the gate, and Elena looked absently out the window again, watching the hubbub of the airport—catering trucks, baggage handlers, other planes shining wet with rain—without really seeing them.

*I decided I ought to give it a chance, though,* she wrote slowly. *That last night, Damon called me brave. Running back home would be just about the farthest thing from brave I can imagine.*

*I* chose *this life, even if I can't remember it.*

*And wherever I live, I'll have to try to figure out how to be normal. Wasn't that something I longed for, all those years?*

*It's not the only thing I ever wanted. Not by a long shot.*

*But it's the only one I've got.*

Up at the front of the plane, the door opened and the other passengers climbed to their feet, surging toward the exit. Elena closed her diary and tucked it in her purse, then stood up and pulled her carry-on out of the overhead bin and, squaring her shoulders, followed the other passengers out of the plane. She was going to be brave.

The airport was crowded with hurrying passengers and, despite being in Paris, managed to have the same soul-deadening atmosphere as any big airport. Fluorescent lighting hummed overhead and the smell of disinfectant was everywhere. There was a headache building up behind Elena's eyes. Maybe she was getting sick. Elena sniffed experimentally, feeling sorry for herself.

Heading for the baggage claim, all at once she saw him, and her whole inside jolted in instant, eager recognition.

No. It was impossible.

But there he was, standing by a magazine stand, looking just the way she remembered him. Strong and graceful and so beautiful, one of the most beautiful people she'd ever seen. He was wearing a beautifully cut black jacket, and he held himself like the aristocrat he'd been born as. Elena couldn't breathe. If she moved, this might be snatched away from her.

Elena knew the exact moment when he saw her, too, and his whole body stiffened in shock. His eyes were wide and his lips were slowly turning up into a smile of amazement.

And then she was in motion, moving straight toward him, her high-heeled boots clacking on the tiled floor, her carry-on rattling along behind her on its little wheels.

He was coming toward her, too, his gaze fixed unwaveringly on her.

*This is it,* Elena realized, stopping stock-still in front of him and staring dumbly up into his face. *This is who I'm meant to be with. My destiny caught up with me after all.*

"Hello, Elena." Damon's mouth twisted into its telltale smirk, and Elena knew she was home.

#TVD13TheEnd

# About the Author

L. J. Smith has written a number of best-selling books and series for young adults, including *The Vampire Diaries* (now a hit TV show), *The Secret Circle*, *The Forbidden Game*, *Night World*, and the *New York Times* #1 bestselling *Dark Visions*. She is happiest sitting by a crackling fire in a cabin in Point Reyes, California, or walking the beaches that surround that area. She loves to hear from readers and hopes they will visit her updated website at www.ljanesmith.net.